"Never thought I'd get my throat cut a second time by them Apaches."

... Curt Degraff said in a level voice. He jerked the heavy Spencer to his shoulder, fired and staggered back a half step because he had not squared himself before shooting. He levered another round into the chamber, pulled back the hammer and waited for another shot.

Slocum squinted into the rising sun, wishing they had found another place to die.... He steadied his rifle on his left hand and balanced against a large boulder. When an Apache poked up, Slocum started to draw back on the trigger, then hesitated. He was glad he had resisted the urge to take a difficult shot. Two other braves burst from cover and dashed forward, hoping their comrade would draw fire away from them.

They were wrong, and they both died under Slocum's deadly aim....

JAKE LOGAN

SLOCUM
AND THE DESERTER

ANNIE'S BOOK STOP
9 MAN MAR DR.
PLAINVILLE, MA 02762
(508) 695-2396

JOVE BOOKS, NEW YORK

SLOCUM AND THE DESERTER

A Jove Book / published by arrangement with
the author

PRINTING HISTORY
Jove edition / March 2002

All rights reserved.
Copyright © 2002 by Penguin Putnam Inc.
This book, or parts thereof, may not be reproduced in any form
without permission.
For information address: The Berkley Publishing Group,
a division of Penguin Putnam Inc.,
375 Hudson Street, New York, New York 10014.

Visit our website at
www.penguinputnam.com

ISBN: 0-515-13265-9

A JOVE BOOK®
Jove Books are published by The Berkley Publishing Group,
a division of Penguin Putnam Inc.,
375 Hudson Street, New York, New York 10014.
JOVE and the "J" design
are trademarks belonging to Penguin Putnam Inc.

PRINTED IN THE UNITED STATES OF AMERICA

10 9 8 7 6 5 4 3 2 1

1

"Everyone's starving to death," Major Cavendish said forcefully, his expression grim. Callused hands clasped in front of him, he leaned forward so much that his battered desk creaked under the strain. "We're starving, disease is running rampant, and if the Apaches attacked right now, there'd be fighting men already half-dead."

John Slocum looked at his partner, Curt Degraff, to see how he was taking the army officer's appraisal of conditions at Fort Selden. New Mexico Territory was never the friendliest of places, not with arid desert, soul-scorching heat and Indians hiding behind every rock, waiting to shoot any white man. And this wasn't even mentioning the rattlers.

"We want to do what's right by you, Major," Degraff said in his gravelly voice. Although he tried to keep it hidden with a ragged blue bandanna, the cause of that harsh speech was apparent in the thin pink scar that went from one ear, across his neck, to the other ear. This reminder of how he had almost died at the knifepoint of an Apache warrior pretty well sealed them to doing the major's bidding.

Slocum wasn't inclined to argue. He and Degraff had

1

teamed up over near the Pecos River in Texas and had drifted around as partners for the better part of two months. He had come to appreciate Degraff's ready humor and fierce fighting ability that had gotten them both out of a couple tight spots. Slocum knew little of Degraff's background. Since the stolid man had not seen fit to tell him much beyond how he had come by the scar on his throat, Slocum didn't reckon it was his place to ask. That Degraff didn't pry into his background made Slocum more comfortable with him as a trail companion.

They understood each other.

"What's right is hunting," the officer said. "We had our rations reduced again." The bitterness in his voice cut like a razor.

"Any part of that due to this being a fort mostly manned by buffalo soldiers?" Degraff asked.

The expression on Cavendish's face told the story. The Army wanted the frontier posts to keep the peace, to hold down Indian raids, to escort stagecoaches and wagon trains, but was only too eager to cut back on money for rations. And when the forts with the black soldiers bought overpriced supplies from local sources, the flour was likely to have weevils in it and the meat riddled with maggots. The worst of it was that the weevils and maggots were more nutritious than the food they lived in.

"How much meat do you want?" Slocum asked, tacitly accepting the job as Fort Selden's hunter.

"Two hundred pounds of fresh meat a week would go a long ways toward keeping the men's bellies from grumbling louder than their mouths," the major said. "Any more than that could be jerked and dried for use on patrol."

Cavendish leaned back in his wobbly desk chair and looked as if he wanted to spit.

"What else?" Slocum asked, seeing the major was having a hard time talking to him and Degraff.

"The pay's not likely to be any good," Cavendish said. "The truth is, I'd be paying you out of my own pocket."

"Don't worry on that score, Major," Degraff said. "We'll be eating just fine while out there running down the deer and bear and anything else with meat on its bones. What more can we ask?"

"Pay," the major said brusquely. "You can ask to be paid, as we all can." He heaved a deep sigh, got to his feet and thrust out his hand for Degraff. "You're both patriots." As he said that, he glanced in Slocum's direction. Slocum's Southern accent was pronounced enough to make the officer wonder about his allegiance.

Slocum didn't bother letting the major know he had fought for the CSA during the war. Those days were long past, and Slocum wanted to forget them. Supplying a fort manned mostly by buffalo soldiers was not a problem for him. Black or white, they deserved rations for the service they provided for the entire territory.

Slocum shook the major's hand and said, "We'd better get after some deer. There's got to be something between here and the Black Range."

"The Caballo Mountains might be a better bet," the major said, "but you have to watch for the Apaches." He laughed harshly. "Truth to tell, you can expect those red bastards to pop up everywhere. They've been on the warpath for months, and nothing we can do gets them back on their reservation."

"We'll keep an eye peeled," Degraff assured the major. He started out of the small office but Slocum hung back.

"Yes. Mr. Slocum?" asked the officer.

"I don't mind not getting paid a lot for this chore," Slocum said, "but we could use some ammunition and maybe a rifle or two. We're a little short on money to buy them over in Mineral Springs."

Major Cavendish chewed on his lower lip, then nodded. "See the armorer and let him know I've authorized you to take the supplies you need. We have to be careful since the War Department cut back on our allocation of gunpowder, too. It's all going south to Fort Davis, thanks to politics. It's not as if we don't have our troubles here."

"Thanks," Slocum said, cutting off the diatribe about how the Fort Davis commander, Colonel Grierson, played on his capture of Satanta to get the lion's share of appropriations.

Slocum hurried after Degraff into the bright New Mexico sun. He squinted a mite, then pulled down the broad brim of his Stetson to shield his eyes as he looked around the cavalry post. The flagpole had broken a couple ropes during the night's high wind and soldiers worked on the high pole to repair it.

"Got that mast from one of them sailing ships out on the Pacific," Degraff said. "They use the same rigging since the wind's so danged powerful here. Not much different from being on a clipper ship headed for the Orient when it comes to force of the wind, no sir."

"What do you know of sailing?" Slocum asked as they crossed the parade ground on their way to the armory.

"Spent time out on the briny," Degraff said. From the way he spoke in a neutral tone Slocum knew better than to ask any more about it. This was another part of Degraff's background that was off limits.

"Get your black asses moving!" shouted a lieutenant at a pair of buffalo soldiers sitting in the shade as they cleaned their rifles. The whip-thin, short lieutenant turned red in the face as he ranted and raved at the soldiers.

Degraff walked past, shaking his head. "Some folks don't know when to keep their mouths shut. That lieutenant's making a powerful lot of enemies. There's only one of him and a hundred of them."

"No reason it should even be 'him' and 'them,'" Slocum said. "But you're right. If he intends to lead anyone in the field, he ought to realize whose ass is likely to be the one getting saved out there."

They went to the armory and looked over the rows of Spencers in their wooden racks. Most of the rifles Slocum didn't give a second glance at because they were in such poor condition, but he found one to his liking.

"That there's Lieutenant Garson's rifle," the armory sergeant said.

"Garson?" Slocum glanced over his shoulder out the door and onto the parade ground where the florid lieutenant marched his two buffalo soldiers back and forth in the hot sun. "That one?" Slocum jerked his thumb in the officer's direction.

"Surely is," the sergeant said with some disdain.

"The rifle's in the best shape of any of them," Degraff said thoughtfully. "Doesn't look to me as if it's ever been fired. It'd be a real pity if one of us didn't take it—on Major Cavendish's orders—to hunt for some fresh meat for the post."

"I saw it first," Slocum said, laying the rifle on the counter and pointing to ammunition for the .50-caliber rifle. "Get one of your own."

"Now, you fellows wouldn't be thinking on asking me to give you the lieutenant's *other* rifle, would you?" The glint in the armorer's eye made it definite. Degraff took the lieutenant's backup rifle. He hefted it, sighted outside at the shouting, sweating bantam rooster of an officer and drew back the trigger. The hammer fell with a hollow click.

"You should check to be sure a rifle's unloaded 'fore you dry fire," the sergeant said uneasily. "You might have shot the lieutenant."

"Fancy that. And if I'm dry firing, then there's no way I can shoot the son of a bitch, now is there?" asked Degraff. He added two boxes of cartridges to the pile Slocum already had and said, "Expect us back with some decent food in a week or so."

"You'd better bring back enough to feed everyone with that much ammo," the sergeant said. "I'd rather give you my gold tooth than four boxes of cartridges. Ammo's more in demand than a decent meal."

"Save your tooth. You'll need it to chomp down on all the venison we'll bring you," Degraff bragged. He hiked the rifle to his shoulder and marched out. Slocum hesitated, then followed as Degraff strutted off mockingly across the parade ground past the cursing Lieutenant Garson. The officer glared at them but did not notice how they had dipped into his personal arsenal.

"Disagreeable cuss," Degraff said. Slocum wasn't going to argue. They went to the livery, saddled their horses and were on the hunt by twilight near a watering hole ten miles away from Fort Selden.

"Two scrawny deers're all we have to show for a day of hunting," grumbled Degraff, picking his teeth with the tip of a wickedly sharp knife. "You'd think they was starving. What's wrong with them? Look around. The desert's had more'n its fair share of rain this year. Greenery everywhere. You'd think dozens of the stupid deer would be nibbling away and getting fat on it."

"They're smarter than that," Slocum said, lounging back on his bedroll. His belly was filled with the first of their kill. Neither deer had dressed out at more than twenty pounds, being hardly more than fawns. "The best grazing if you're a deer is up in the mountains, not down here. We're lucky to have found these."

"We'll dry the meat while we're doing some real hunting," Degraff vowed. He belched, spat a piece of gristle and then took a deep drink of the coffee Slocum had brewed. Degraff smiled broadly. "The only good thing about being partners with you is that you know how to make drinkable coffee."

"Thanks," Slocum said dryly. He lay back and stared up at the night sky, blinking when a shooting star flashed across. His mind drifted, wondering if they ought to take even this small amount of venison back to the fort before continuing their hunt. The few pounds were hardly worth the trip back since they wouldn't give every man at Fort Selden more than a couple ounces. Better to bag a significant amount to justify claiming so much precious ammunition.

Slocum sat bolt upright and stared at Degraff, who swung his knife around and gripped it firmly. Putting his finger to his lips, signaling for silence, Slocum got to his feet and slipped out the Colt Navy slung in its cross-draw holster. On cat's feet he faded into shadows and went prowling to find the cause of the small sound both he and Degraff had heard.

Walking carefully amid the Spanish bayonet threatening to poke through the soles of his boots or to drive its sharp points into his legs, Slocum left the camp behind quickly. A few thirsty cottonwoods provided shelter near the watering hole, but a dozen yards beyond lay mostly desert plants. The Spanish bayonets, huge, mountainous clumps of prickly pear cactus, whiplike ocotillos, and ankle-high buffalo grass, provided little cover. Slocum kept low to keep from silhouetting himself against the bright stars, but he quickly tired of making his way hunched over.

As he stood to his full six-foot height, he heard a sound matching the one that had alerted him. He turned slowly and gradually located the noise. Without hesitation, he aimed his six-shooter and fired. He was rewarded with a loud yelp of pain and a string of curses.

In Apache.

Slocum didn't stand around congratulating himself. He

had only winged the Apache warrior sneaking up on their camp and wasn't about to go chasing after him into the darkness. He hightailed it back to where Degraff stood with his rifle ready for action.

"Apaches?" his partner asked.

Slocum nodded.

"Damned Apaches aren't supposed to attack at night," Degraff said, packing up his belongings and getting ready to strike camp.

"If they're desperate enough, they'll risk getting rattlesnake bit," Slocum said, his gear already stashed and his saddlebags ready to fling over the rump of his gelding.

"We can't be that easy a' pickings for them," grumbled Degraff. He cinched the belly strap down tight and checked his saddle. His mare neighed and shied away. Degraff didn't try to control it because he knew what spooked the skittish horse. He spun, his rifle coming up. He fired into shadows and was rewarded with an anguished cry that died quickly.

"You got him," Slocum said. He knew the sound of a man dying. Degraff had just killed an Apache brave.

"Let's clear out before they circle us," Degraff said. "How many do you reckon there are?"

"One less, thanks to your shooting" was all Slocum said. His gelding bucked as he mounted. Slocum looked around, thought he saw a safe way out of their camp and headed for it, quickly learning how wrong he was. He had not counted on so many Apaches lying in ambush. An arrow sang through the still night air and cut the brim of his Stetson. Slocum flinched and put his spurs to the horse's flanks. With a leap, the gelding cleared the barricade of Apache warriors ahead of it and thundered blindly away from the watering hole.

Slocum slowed a few minutes later, afraid the horse might step into a prairie dog hole in the darkness and break a leg. He turned and looked over his shoulder to see Degraff close behind.

"We should have realized more than deer would come to a sweet water oasis like that," Slocum said.

"The Apaches might cotton to the taste of venison, too," Degraff said. "That could explain why we only got a couple small deer."

Slocum cocked his head to one side and listened hard. He didn't believe what he heard.

"They're chasing us!"

"Son of a bitch!" grumbled Degraff. "Why don't they give up and go to sleep?"

"Something's got them really riled," Slocum said, "and they intend taking it out on us." He wondered if the Apache war party thought they might be scouts from Fort Selden intent on bringing the bluecoats down on their necks. Whatever the reason, Apaches, who normally were fearful about fighting at night, were on their trail.

Slocum silently cut away from the route they had taken, circled and began using every bit of his skill to lose the pursuing Indians. In their months together Slocum had quickly determined that he was far better a frontiersman than Curt Degraff. The man was a decent hunter, but when it came to covering his trail or tracking, he was little better than a greenhorn.

They rode in silence, Degraff going where Slocum indicated and Slocum using his wiles to keep the Apaches off their tail. But every time Slocum thought they were safe, he heard the unmistakable sounds of pursuit. Through the night they kept on the go, until the faint light of dawn lit the land.

"My mare's too tuckered out to go a step farther," Degraff called to Slocum. "We either rest or the horse dies under me."

Slocum's gelding was similarly exhausted. Reluctantly

he began hunting for a place where they could make a stand.

"The Apaches are less than a mile behind us. With sunup, they'll spot us quick."

"It's good we didn't find too many deer, then," Degraff said wryly. "We've still got enough ammo left to acquit ourselves well."

Slocum wanted to get away without a fight but saw this was out of the question. Like an inexorable tide, the Apaches narrowed the distance between them. Slocum pulled the Spencer to his shoulder, steadied himself and got off a shot that spooked his gelding. But the bullet flew true and knocked the leading brave from horseback.

"We need some more of your fine shooting, Slocum." Degraff swore under his breath when he saw a half dozen more warriors replace the one who had been shot.

"Looks as if we're up against the whole damned Apache tribe," Slocum said. "There. Up on the rise are a few rocks we can use."

"Those pebbles? We might as well chuck them at the Apaches as hide behind them," Degraff said, but he was already cruelly spurring his tired horse up the slope to where they'd make a stand.

Slocum hoped it wouldn't be their last stand.

2

"Never thought I'd end up getting my throat cut a second time by them Apaches," Curt Degraff said in a level voice. He jerked the heavy Spencer to his shoulder, fired and staggered back a half step because he had not squared himself before shooting. He levered another round into the chamber, pulled back the hammer and waited for another shot.

Slocum squinted into the rising sun, wishing they had found another place to die. It was hot and it was miserable here. But then he had never really thought about where he would finally meet his maker. He had taken life one day at a time and never worried about what tomorrow would bring.

He steadied his rifle on his left hand and balanced against a large boulder. When an Apache poked up, Slocum started to draw back on the trigger, then hesitated. He was glad he had resisted the urge to take a difficult shot. Two other braves burst from cover and dashed forward, hoping their comrade would draw fire away from them.

They were wrong, and they both died under Slocum's deadly aim.

11

"It's like dipping water from the ocean with a tea-spoon," observed Degraff. "Shoot one, two more pop up." He fired again and missed.

Slocum looked around for the hundredth time, hoping something had changed. It had not. They were in the middle of a ring of rocks atop a rise. The steep slope forced the Apaches to come at them slower than if they were out in the open, but that was about their only advantage. The chest-high rocks afforded scant protection, their horses had run off the first chance they got, and with them went supplies and water. Already Slocum's mouth was cottony and the thought of even a sip of tepid water was like paradise.

"They can wait us out," Slocum said, shielding his eyes from the new morning. "They know we'll die of thirst in a day or two. The sun's on their side, so why are they attacking?"

"Gotcha, you red varmint!" crowed Degraff. He drew back his smoking rifle and worked to reload the tubular magazine in the stock.

Slocum switched to cover their back and discovered a half dozen Apaches had almost reached the top of the hill behind them. He fired until his rifle came up empty, then whipped out his six-shooter and emptied that, eventually driving back four warriors. He reloaded as fast as he could and was almost overrun again.

"You got any ideas about that?" Slocum called.

"About what?"

"Why don't they wait for us to die instead of coming at us like this? We've accounted for quite a few of them, but they aren't pulling back."

"Maybe they're just mad at all white eyes and want to take it out on us," suggested Degraff.

That didn't set well with Slocum. The Apaches were no man's fools. They were fierce fighters and knew when to fall back. Waiting for the sun to boil his and Degraff's

brains was the smart thing to do, but the Indians kept up
a steady attack. They had to know there wasn't anything
worth stealing off the two men's dead bodies, and scalps
were not that important to an Apache, even one pissed as
hell.

Slocum got off three more quick shots, all misses. He
was running low on ammo and saw Degraff had spent his
two boxes even faster. It was only a matter of time before
the fighting became hand to hand, and he and his partner
died.

"Yeow!" cried Degraff. Slocum looked over his shoulder and saw his partner's arm turn red. When Degraff
turned slightly, he showed where he had taken an arrow.

"Don't pull it out. It's got a barbed hunting tip," Slocum cautioned. He fired twice more, then went to Degraff's side. Gripping the arrow firmly, he pushed it
through the man's shoulder. Degraff turned pale and wob-
bled, but Slocum finally got the arrowhead through. He
snapped it off, and jerked the shaft out. He ripped away
part of Degraff's shirt and pressed it into the wound.

"Hold it as tight as you can," Slocum said, scooping
up his partner's dropped rifle.

"I'm getting kinda dizzy, John," Degraff said. "Don't
let them take me. Use the next to last bullet on me."

"I'll use them all on the Apaches," Slocum said coldly.
He would die fighting and would never take his own
life—or his partner's. With well-placed shots he brought
down another brave, then tossed aside his rifle and drew
Degraff's to his shoulder.

"Behind," came Degraff's weak warning.

Slocum ducked, whirled and fired point-blank into an
Indian's belly. The heavy slug lifted the Apache and threw
him back into another warrior.

Slocum tried to fire at the second Indian, but the rifle
was empty. He whipped out the thick-bladed knife he car-

ried in a sheath at the small of his back and dived into
the fray.

Blood flew like raindrops in a storm. When the fighting
was over, Slocum stood bloodied from head to foot but
still alive.

"They're really comin' for us now," Degraff grated out.
"So much shooting. What a send-off to the Promised
Land."

Slocum chanced a quick look over the top of the rock
where Degraff had sunk down, still clutching his shoulder.
For a few seconds he didn't see anything. Then his heart
almost exploded at the sight of two blue uniformed men
on foot running fearlessly into the Apache ranks. He
wanted to warn them this was suicide, then saw it was
only a diversion. A dozen more soldiers attacked from the
Apache flank.

The Apaches broke and ran, chased by the soldiers.
Slocum sank down, wiped gore from his face and then
used his bandanna to get more off his hands. He didn't
want his grip slipping if he had to use his knife until the
buffalo soldiers rescued him and Degraff.

"What's going on?" Degraff asked.

"Salvation," Slocum said. "In blue uniforms." He
looked up to see a giant of a man towering over him. For
all his size, the black sergeant had moved like a ghost up
the back of the hill. Slocum had been keyed up and waiting for more Apaches, and the soldier had still sneaked
up on him.

"You two look like death," the sergeant said.

"And you look like an angel," Degraff said, grinning.
"A big, black one, but still a right purty angel of mercy."

"Don't you go thinkin' 'bout kissin' me," the sergeant
grumbled. "You hurt bad?" He dropped to one knee and
expertly examined Degraff's wound. "Nah, you'll live to
lie 'bout how you run off Dark Crow's entire band."

"He the Apache war chief?" asked Slocum.

"Of this band. There's a half dozen different bucks tryin' to be top dog but he's 'bout the orneriest of the lot." The sergeant glanced at Slocum and asked. "Any of that your blood? Didn't think so."

Slocum sheathed his knife and reached for the Spencer he had dropped. A huge black hand clamped around his wrist and kept him from taking the rifle.

"What you doin' with Army rifles?"

"We're not gunrunners," Slocum said. "Major Cavendish hired us to hunt for meat to supply Fort Selden."

"For the cavalry, eh? Fort Selden?"

"You out of the fort? Or maybe you hail from Fort Bayard?" asked Degraff.

"Save your strength," Slocum said. "The sergeant's from Fort Selden. I recognize the Ninth Cavalry insignia."

"You got a sharp eye, mister. You ever in the Army?" asked the sergeant, studying Slocum closely.

"I wasn't a Federal," Slocum said, wanting to drop the matter. "Now I'm working for Cavendish, as I said."

"I'm Benjamin Washington, sergeant, H Company," the huge man said, thrusting out a grimy hand the size of a ham.

Slocum shook, introducing himself and Degraff.

"You got any objection to returning to the fort?" Sergeant Washington asked, still wary of them. Any indication they wanted to remain would deepen the sergeant's suspicion of some illegal activity. Having the two Army rifles had planted the seeds in his mind.

"Not if the post sawbones is any good," Slocum said. "My friend's in bad shape."

"Seen worse," Washington said, shrugging. "He's strong." The black sergeant turned and put his fingers in his mouth and let loose with an ear-splitting whistle. "We'll run down your mounts and get you started on the trail."

"Will you be riding with us?" asked Degraff.

"Reckon so. This patrol's about over. We done all the mischief we can." Washington waved to his men down the hill and waited patiently as they made their way up. One private stared at Slocum and Degraff with wide eyes.

"What's wrong, Farmer?" asked the sergeant.

"They killed danged near half of Dark Crow's braves. Jist the two of 'em!"

Sergeant Washington looked at Slocum with new respect.

"Why were the Apaches so intent on killing us?" Slocum asked. "They could have waited us out instead of giving us good targets as they attacked."

"Dark Crow'd never give anybody a good target," denied Washington. "As to why he wanted you, might be that he thought you were scouts and had found his camp. We been lookin' for it goin' on a month."

"There's a watering hole a ways back," Slocum said. "but the Apaches never camp at one. They'd be a mile or so away, to keep from scaring off the game and to protect their water source."

"You know a bit 'bout them. Might be we ought to hire you as a scout 'stead of a hunter?"

Slocum laughed without humor. He might as well act as scout since he and Degraff had done so poorly as hunters. Slocum wished his brother Robert were here. He had been a good hunter before the war took his life.

"They got some fresh meat packed out, Sarge," called a corporal, leading Slocum and Degraff's horses.

"How much?" The question was sharp. Slocum knew the answer would mean the difference between going to the post in chains or as free men.

"Twenty-thirty pounds all dressed out. Looks to me as if they was fixin' on sellin' it," said the corporal.

"Or taking it back to Fort Selden," Washington said. He ran a strong arm around Degraff's shoulders and lifted the man easily, then boosted him into the saddle. "Let's get on back and sample some of Mr. Slocum's fresh-shot venison!"

They rode into Fort Selden a little past noon two days later. Curt Degraff had slowed them but not too much. Slocum heaved a sigh of relief when the post surgeon rushed out to see if anyone in Washington's patrol required medical aid and helped Degraff to the infirmary.

"Get the meat over to the cook," Slocum said, pointing toward the mess hall. "I should check in with the major."

"I need to report, too," Sergeant Washington said, handing the reins of his horse to a private. The two had started across the parade ground under the flagpole when a sharp command froze Washington in his tracks. Slocum was slower to turn since he knew the source of the disturbance.

"Sergeant Washington," growled the short, thin officer who had given his soldiers hell before. "What's the meaning of this?"

"I don't understand, Lieutenant Garson," drawled Washington. "I'm on my way to report to the major."

"You report to me," Garson said, coming around and staring up at Washington. The lieutenant jutted out his chin and bumped his chest against Washington's. It was all Slocum could do to keep from laughing when the officer bounced off, as if Washington was an immense granite statue.

"Well, then. Lieutenant. I'm back. We can all go to the major so's I can tell what I found."

"You will report to *me*," Garson said, his voice turning shrill. Slocum started to speak but a quick sidelong glance from Washington made him hold his tongue. "I know why you want to talk to the major. It's because you have done nothing while on patrol. You and your shiftless men went out, found a watering hole and sat there the entire while."

"He saved my hide, Lieutenant," Slocum said, unable

to listen to such baseless accusations any longer. "My partner and I got pinned down by Dark Crow's band and—"

"I didn't speak to you," Garson said in his nasty tone. He turned back to Washington, who stood stolidly. "You will report, Sergeant. Now!"

"Didn't accomplish much, Lieutenant," Washington said. "Dark Crow's been leadin' us a merry chase. Engaged some of his braves once or twice, but they always kept away from my patrol."

"As I thought. You ought to be court-martialed for dereliction of duty, but the major would never permit it. He is too softhearted when it comes to dealing with your kind."

"What's that mean, Lieutenant?" asked Slocum, moving closer. "You mean noncoms? Enlisted soldiers? Or do you mean something else?"

Garson stepped away from Washington and rested his hand on the heavy cavalry saber at his hip. Slocum had rarely seen any officer carry one in the field since they were ineffectual weapons against rifles and bows and arrows. Somehow, it did not surprise him that Garson affected one.

"Sergeant, you are restricted to post until further notice."

"But Lieutenant, I—"

"Say another word and I'll have your stripes and throw you in the guardhouse," Garson said.

"You can order him around, but not me," Slocum said. He had heard enough to know Garson was not the sort to fight out in the open. If he pushed the lieutenant too much, he would retaliate against Washington and the buffalo soldiers in his company in ways Slocum could not counter. Slocum had to make this personal between him and the officer to keep the soldier out of it.

"I'll have you thrown into the stocks," Garson threat-cned.

"Do it after I talk to the post commander," Slocum said, pushing past Garson. He made sure he shouldered the man hard enough to knock him back a step or two. Slocum let the lieutenant bluster as he went to the major's office on the far side of the parade ground.

"He's not there!" called Garson. "The major's gone to Fort Thorn to meet with Colonel Hatch. I am in command of Fort Selden until he returns!"

Slocum turned, stared coldly at Garson, then spat. Without another word, he changed direction and headed for the infirmary to see how Degraff was doing. There would be time to set things right when Cavendish returned.

He entered the dim, cool building and looked back to see Garson still dressing down Washington.

"He's a pistol, isn't he?"

Slocum saw a captain holding a pan of water and looking past him, to where Garson continued his truculent verbal attack on the sergeant.

"Why aren't you in charge? He's only a lieutenant," Slocum said. but he knew the reason. Chain of command. Garson was a field officer. The doctor was not. In matters medical, the captain held sway, but Garson supposedly knew how to defend the fort and lead men, not just patch them up.

"He only thinks he is in charge," the captain said, laughing. "Sergeant Washington there runs things and does a danged good job of it." The captain gave Slocum the once-over and said, "Any of that blood yours?"

"Not much," Slocum allowed. "You have somewhere I can take a bath?"

"Praise be," the doctor said. "A man at Fort Selden who actually *wants* to bathe. Out back. The water's been out in the sun all day so it's already hot."

Slocum felt worlds better after washing off the blood caking his skin. Getting the blood out of his clothing proved almost impossible so he had to put on his spare shirt and jeans. Otherwise, he would have looked like a clumsy slaughterhouse worker. By the time he spent some time with Degraff and had chowed down in the mess hall, it was getting dark.

Walking around the post, Slocum saw that Garson had doubled the usual number of sentries. He wondered if Washington had put the fear of Dark Crow's warriors into the lieutenant or if Garson had some other reason. Whatever it was, Slocum didn't intend leaving Fort Selden until Degraff was able to ride.

He sat on the steps of the infirmary and enjoyed the cool desert night air as he thought on whether he and Degraff ought to hunt some more for the major or move on. As he considered what was in his own best interest, Slocum saw a huge shadow detach itself from the barracks nearby and move toward the waist-high adobe wall circling the fort.

More curious than alarmed, he followed. The man reached the wall, waited until the guards were looking in other directions, then flowed over to the outside as silent as a puff of night breeze.

Slocum recognized Benjamin Washington and wondered where the sergeant was going in such a secretive way. Then he realized he was not alone in seeing the sergeant go over the wall.

Lieutenant Garson sneered, rested his hand on the hilt of his saber and strutted off, whistling tunelessly as he left.

3

"Are you sure it was Washington you saw sneaking out last night?" Degraff asked. He lay propped up in bed, looking more like his former self after a twelve-hour sleep and a few yards of bandage and tape on his shoulder.

"It's mighty hard to mistake a man the size of Washington. He might have been going into town, but Garson also saw him."

"That little pissant needs to be put into his place," Degraff said angrily. "He wasn't out there gettin' his balls blowed off. Sergeant Washington saved us."

"The lieutenant had no call restricting Washington to the post, but until Cavendish returns, I don't see what we can do about it. Garson is in charge."

"Damned fool," grumbled Degraff.

Slocum went to the window in the surgery and peered out. He sucked in his breath when he figured out the drama being enacted out on the parade grounds.

"I've got to go. Be back in a while," Slocum said, not waiting for Degraff to ask what was so all fired important. Slocum hurried outside and across the dusty grounds to the stocks mounted on a sturdy wood post near the flag-pole.

"I ought to court-martial you for desertion," Garson shouted at Washington, "but that would be too easy. You'd be cashiered and sent on your way. There wouldn't be any punishment for your crime."

"Lieutenant, what's going on?" asked Slocum, knowing full well what was happening. Garson had caught Washington when he returned to the fort after his nocturnal escape.

"You butt out," Garson snapped. "I have business to tend to. Official business."

Slocum started to protest but saw the look on Washington's face and fell silent. The time for speaking out would come when he had Major Cavendish's ear. Nothing he said now would deter Garson.

"You are a miserable cur, a deserter who jeopardized the safety of the fort and everyone in it." Garson's lips were dotted with spittle as he worked himself into a rage. He stood a pace away from the hulking Benjamin Washington and even then seemed dwarfed by Washington's size and authority. "I'm not going to court-martial you. I'm going to give you another chance to be a real soldier."

"Thank you, sir," Washington said with just a hint of sarcasm in his voice. He stared straight ahead over the top of Garson's garrison cap.

"You will be given corporal punishment this very instant. Twenty lashes!"

"What?" Washington's eyes widened. "You can't do that. The major said he wouldn't tolerate that."

"The major is not in command. I am!" Garson motioned for four privates to grab Washington. If the sergeant had shrugged his mighty shoulders. He would have sent them flying like skittle pins. He let the privates strip off his blue uniform shirt but struggled when they started to put him in the stocks.

With an incoherent cry of rage, Garson swung the whip he held in his hands. The lash caught Washington squarely across the back and knocked him to his knees.

Slocum had reached the end of his patience. He took two quick steps, measured the distance and unloaded a haymaker that caught Garson smack in the belly. The lieutenant gasped at the blow, bent double and gagged.

"Don't do that to him," Slocum said. Garson was on the ground on hands and knees, retching. "He saved my partner and me yesterday."

"Mr. Slocum, don't," Washington cautioned. The welt from the whip across his broad dusky back pulsed visibly.

Slocum turned to face Garson again as the officer struggled to get to his feet.

"You are a miserable son of a bitch treating any man in your command this way," Slocum said. He had been a captain in the CSA and knew the importance of discipline. He also knew the men under your command deserved some respect if they were to fight for you in the field.

"G-get this man to the guardhouse," gasped out Garson. The privates hesitated but a dozen more had come up to see what the fuss was about. Slocum looked around at the black faces, turning from him to Washington and back. Only when another white officer came up did the tableau shift—and it went against Slocum.

"You heard Lieutenant Garson's order," bellowed the new officer. "Get that civilian to the guardhouse. And give this man twenty lashes."

"Twenty additional lashes," Garson said, swallowing hard as he got his wind back. "See to Slocum, Lieutenant Porter, and I'll tend to our wayward nigger!"

Slocum tried to deck Garson again, but this time soldiers caught his arms and held him. Lieutenant Porter sneered, then motioned in the direction of the guardhouse. As they dragged him to the stockade, Slocum heard Garson's whip cutting into Washington's back. Slocum could not see the sergeant, but he flinched with every loud crack and moan dragged from Washington's lips.

• • •

The key in the lock brought Slocum up from the rude cot where he had spent the past four days. If Garson or his lackey Porter had opened the door, Slocum would have punched him again, but standing in the narrow doorway was Curt Degraff, Major Cavendish beside him.

"You should choose your fights more carefully, Mr. Slocum," the major said. "The lieutenant wanted you in front of a firing squad."

"He shouldn't have—"

Cavendish held up his hand to silence Slocum's angry outburst. "Lieutenant Garson might not be the best officer in this man's army, nor is Lieutenant Porter, but they're all I've got."

"You've got good men in the ranks. Don't let your officers—"

"Slocum," snapped the major. "Keep your mouth shut or I'll lock you up and throw away the key. Mr. Degraff has convinced me to release you, in spite of Garson's protests and against my own better judgment."

"Truth is, they got Apache problems and might need us to scout," Degraff said, grinning. He looked hale and hearty after his rest in the post infirmary.

"That is, uh, correct," Cavendish said reluctantly. "Dark Crow seems intent on committing more outrages than Victorio to gain prestige and win control of the Warm Springs Apache. I need to put a stop to Dark Crow's predations immediately. The settlers are getting uneasy every time they see an Indian."

"We'll do our best, Major," Degraff said. "From outside your fine stockade."

"Yes, well, see that you steer clear of Garson. I need both of you."

With that the major left to speak to the jailer. He pointed back at Slocum, then signed an order releasing him.

"I got you out without so much as a black mark on your record," Degraff said, laughing.

"Thanks. Given a chance, Garson would have had me in front of that firing squad," Slocum said.

"No, he'd have insisted on a necktie party! That way he could let you swing in the wind for a week so the buzzards could dine on your putrid flesh 'fore pukin' it back up."

"You've got a way with words," Slocum said, leaving the stockade and stepping into the bright sun for the first time since Garson had ordered him locked up. "What happened to Washington?"

"He took his twenty lashes," Degraff said, turning somber. "Garson took his stripes and fined him six months' pay."

"The son of a bitch," muttered Slocum.

"The Army's full of 'em," Degraff said. "Fort Selden just has more than its share. If you think Garson is bad, you ought to hear Porter talk."

"Cavendish ought to relieve them of duty," Slocum said, but he knew the reason the major did nothing. Getting any officer was difficult for black units. Commanding buffalo soldiers was considered by many to be punishment duty for white officers. Custer had turned down a promotion because it would have meant commanding black soldiers.

Slocum knew Garson and Porter might end up like Custer if they didn't identify their real enemy. Dark Crow sounded intent on becoming a war chief leading hundreds of Apaches into battle, and if he wasn't stopped he would soak the deserts of New Mexico Territory in blood.

"There's Washington," Slocum said, seeing the big man out in the sun.

Washington was stripped to the waist, showing the prominent weals across his back. As he sweat, the salty perspiration running across the welts had to sting like fire. Seeing this made Slocum even angrier.

"You shouldn't talk to him," Degraff warned. "It'll only get you both into more trouble."

Slocum ignored his partner and went to where Washington raked the parade ground clear of small pebbles.

"Sergeant Washington," Slocum called. The big man looked up and glared at him.

"You shouldn't be talkin' to me," Washington said.

"I tried to stop him. What Garson did was—"

"Go away," Washington said harshly. "We'll all get into more trouble if you don't." The black man looked past Slocum, then sullenly went back to raking.

"Slocum, can I have a word with you?" Lieutenant Garson came strutting up. "We got off on the wrong foot, you and I. Let's work out our differences, man to man. Southerner to Southerner, if I peg your accent right. Where are you from? Georgia? I'm from Alabama."

Slocum turned and looked down at the man. His mind went blank. Slocum was jolted back to his senses when his right hand began to hurt. He looked down at his fist and realized it hurt because he had decked Garson again. The lieutenant lay sprawled on his back, knocked out from Slocum's single punch to his chin.

"John, come along. We might consider moseying on," Degraff said, taking Slocum's arm and pulling him away. "I'm not saying Garson didn't deserve it. I'd be happy to beat up on him myself, if my shoulder was in better shape, but the major's going to stretch your neck if you keep this up."

Degraff rattled on as he led Slocum away. All around the fort came murmurs of approval. Garson was not well liked among the buffalo soldiers, but Slocum realized he was treading on dangerous ground. The major could not allow this attack to go unpunished since it was bad for discipline.

"We're not that important to Cavendish, are we?" Slocum asked.

"Nope," Degraff said cheerily. He released Slocum, turned and sat on the steps leading up into the infirmary. Degraff motioned for Slocum to join him. "Let's see what happens."

Garson was struggling back to consciousness. He pushed up to an elbow, then got to shaky feet. The lieutenant took a step, faltered and then turned in a full circle as if trying to figure out where he was.

"Don't think he knows what happened," Degraff said softly. Behind them the doctor came from the infirmary.

"Has Garson been out in the sun too long again?" the captain asked.

"You might go see," Degraff said. "I'd let my partner go, but he's got a sore hand and ought to rest." Degraff laughed uproariously. The captain stared at him, not understanding, shrugged and went to see if Garson needed help.

"You're one lucky son of a buck," Degraff said when it became apparent Slocum had hit Garson so hard that it had punched loose all memory of what happened. From the way the buffalo soldiers who had been watching moved away like dust on the wind, it seemed they weren't likely to peach on Slocum. Benjamin Washington leaned on the rake and watched in silence as the captain led Garson to the infirmary.

"You must have hit your chin when you fell," the doctor was saying as he and Garson went past Slocum and Degraff.

"I've never got sunstroke before," Garson said, still groggy.

"It happens if you get left out in the noonday heat too long," Degraff called after them. "You need to take special care if you're sensitive to the heat!" He grabbed his sides as he laughed heartily.

Slocum didn't share his partner's glee. He watched as Washington continued his solitary punishment detail out in the sun, never speeding up but never stopping, either. He was a soldier doing what he was ordered to do, even if the order was cruel.

"We have time to take a little siesta before chow," Degraff said. "They've gone through all the venison we brought in, but we can bag more when we're out scouting. I reckon the major'll give us ten dollars a month."

"If he can steal that much from his troops' pay," Slocum said.

"So we don't get paid. We still get fed."

What passed for victuals at Fort Selden turned Slocum's stomach, but he let Degraff lead the way to the mess hall. They sat in the shade, drinking water and waiting for the evening meal. Slocum saw the way the buffalo soldiers clustered at the rear of the hall, letting Slocum, Degraff and the white officers have a table to themselves. Slocum wanted to see how Washington was doing but refrained from asking. Washington sat away from the others, as if he were as much of a maverick as the whites.

"Finally," Degraff said, looking outside. "The danged sun's going down. That means we can get some relief from the heat."

A sluggish breeze blew off the desert and then turned chilly as the sand and rock gave up all their heat in a rush. When they'd done eating, Slocum and Degraff sat on unused rain barrels outside the livery and enjoyed the cool after the day's intense heat.

"We should go curry our horses," Degraff said. "They were grateful enough that we fed them this morning."

"There's plenty of time," Slocum said. "Rest up. Don't open that wound in your shoulder."

"I'm thinking we ought to take the horses and ride out of here," Degraff said. "We can't do anything about Dark

Crow, and the way things are going in Fort Selden, you might get yourself lynched."

"We promised Major Cavendish we'd help out against the Apaches," Slocum said. "When we get on the trail, it'll be different."

"Yeah, different," grumbled Degraff. "The Apaches will be shooting at us again."

"You can ride on. Albuquerque's only a week to the north."

"And let you get into trouble with Garson again? You need my held to stay out of the stockade, Slocum." Degraff's good humor had returned. He joshed Slocum some more, then they went into the livery stable to tend their horses. It was almost time for the bugler to sound taps when they finished and stepped outside.

"Do me a favor, Slocum, and roll me a smoke. I'm still a bit gimpy."

Degraff held out his left arm and winced at the movement. Slocum wasn't sure how much was acting and how much was real. What he saw was how unlikely it was that his partner wasn't dexterous enough to roll a cigarette.

"I suppose you want me to use my own tobacco, too," Slocum said, already taking out the fixings from his shirt pocket. He worked to build a smoke, then passed it to Degraff. As he fumbled for a lucifer, he heard someone behind the livery. Slocum and Degraff exchanged looks.

"Who do you figure is out at this time of night?" Degraff asked. He tucked the cigarette behind his ear and went to investigate.

"Careful," Slocum warned. "The major said Dark Crow was kicking up a fuss."

"We know that already. What Apache is going to come into Fort Selden at night?"

"Who'd have thought the Apaches would have chased us all night long?" Slocum shot back. He followed his partner in the dark, catching his toe on a half-buried rock and pitching forward.

The clumsiness saved his life. Slocum flailed for balance as a shot rang out. He hit the ground and looked up. Curt Degraff stood stock-still in front of him. He twisted around and then sank to the ground without making a sound.

Slocum scrambled to his partner on hands and knees. Degraff was dead. Whipping out his six-shooter, Slocum looked around for the man who had murdered his partner.

Faint footsteps sounded behind the stable. Slocum swung around and pointed his six-gun at the corner of the building just as Benjamin Washington came around. The soldier clutched a pistol in his hand. Slocum started to shoot but held back as thudding boots came up behind him.

Slocum glanced back to see Lieutenant Garson with his six-shooter out and pointed at Washington.

"Murderer!" cried Garson as he opened fire. Washington ducked back behind the stables. The lieutenant ran forward and bumped into Slocum. Both men tumbled to the ground in a tangle of arms and legs.

"You fool! Let me up!" shouted Garson.

Seconds later horses' hooves echoed off into the night, faded quickly and then left behind only the sound of the pint-sized officer cursing his bad luck.

4

Slocum thought half the troopers in the Fort Selden garrison surrounded them. Garson yelled, thrashed about and finally got his feet under him.

"Get after him!" Garson shrieked.

"Who might that be, suh?" asked Private Farmer, still pulling on his pants.

"Washington, that's who. He shot that fellow and took off. He's on the run. I knew he was a killer!"

Slocum went to Degraff's side and rolled the man over. He had been dead when he hit the ground. The bullet had cut clean through his heart. Slocum stared at the bloody spot on Degraff's chest and touched it with his fingertips. Then he rolled his partner over and looked at his back.

"The bullet hit him from behind," Slocum said.

"That makes it even worse," Garson said. "Washington's a backshooting son of a bitch!"

Slocum tried to figure out what had happened. Degraff had died fast, so fast the cigarette was still tucked over his ear where he had put it when they had heard the noise behind the livery.

"He was shot from the direction of the parade ground," Slocum said suddenly. He realized that he would be the one lying dead on the ground if he had not clumsily tripped and fallen.

"Nonsense," said Garson. "Washington shot him from the rear of the livery. Your partner must have seen the danger and turned to warn you as Washington fired."

"Then Washington didn't mean to shoot Degraff in the back," Slocum said.

"It's still murder. What are you, a bunkhouse lawyer trying to get the killer off? That's your *partner,* Slocum. He's dead! Don't you feel any outrage that he was shot down in front of your eyes?"

Slocum was pushed aside as a squad of buffalo soldiers swarmed past, on their way to find Washington's trail. Some got their horses from the stables, but Garson didn't give any command for them to mount and go after the fugitive.

Watching the bustle, Slocum came to a slow conclusion—but he was certain it was the right one. Degraff had been shot in the back by a bullet meant for Slocum. And Washington had been out of sight in back of the livery when Degraff died. That meant the only man behind Slocum was the killer.

Garson.

Slocum knew why the lieutenant had not fired a second time to finish the job he had botched the first time. He had intended to kill Slocum, but the first shot had brought nervous soldiers running. The major had instilled fear of an Apache attack in all of them. Most probably slept with one eye open, hand on a rifle as they waited for Dark Crow to come after them in their bunks.

Garson finally got his men assembled and ready for pursuit, then turned and stared straight at Slocum.

"You gonna lead the hunt, Slocum? Didn't the major hire you as a scout? I'd think a man of your upbringing would want to catch your own partner's killer." Garson refused to stop the badgering. Slocum knew how a fox with a hound on its trail felt.

"I know who killed Degraff," he said. "All I need to know is why." His cold green eyes locked on Garson's watery blue ones. For a moment, the lieutenant held the gaze, then he looked away to bark orders to his troopers.

"After him, men. We got a killer to run down. No quarter, if you spot him. Shoot first." Garson took the reins of his horse from his striker and mounted. He glared at Slocum for a moment, then wheeled his horse around and gave the order for the bugler to sound the column's advance.

Slocum saddled his gelding and got to the middle of the parade ground when he heard a sharp command that froze him in place. It also stopped Garson and the company with him.

"Mr. Garson!" bellowed Major Cavendish. "Where the hell are you going? I have given you no orders to mount your troopers!"

"Sir, we're after a killer. Washington shot a scout in the back and we're after him."

"Washington?" Cavendish frowned and shook his head. "That doesn't sound like him."

"He—"

"Quiet," Cavendish said, silencing the junior officer with a hand motion like an ax chopping wood. "I can't have you traipsing off in the night like this, not with Dark Crow out there. Besides, I have a mission for you. Come sunup, you and your company'll ride north to the Wilkinson place. He's spotted Apaches lurking around and is worried he'll have both his horses and cattle stolen."

"Sir, capturing Washington is important. He's on the run. If we let him go—"

"You weren't listening, Lieutenant. Protecting a settler and his family is more important than a deserter, even one accused of murder. I intend to prevent not only theft from

Mr. Wilkinson but also his women being stolen and his scalp lifted by Dark Crow."

Garson's mouth opened and then closed like a beached fish. He saluted smartly and dismissed his troop, with orders to assemble a half hour before dawn to ride to the settler's spread.

Slocum remained in the saddle as Cavendish ordered Garson to his office for more detailed orders. He knew what had happened but could not prove it. Cavendish would see that Curt Degraff was dead but would accept his officer's word about the circumstances over that of a civilian he hardly knew.

Cavendish had thought highly of Washington. With the deserter's testimony along with Slocum's suspicions, Garson might go in front of a firing squad for backshooting Degraff. Slocum put his heels to his horse's flanks and left Fort Selden behind, slowly riding in a fan pattern to find fresh tracks.

Following Benjamin Washington in the dark was hard, but Slocum was driven by a fire in his gut to settle the score with Garson. If anyone had reason to hate the lieutenant more, Slocum knew it had to be Washington. Their combined testimony might not be enough to convince a jury, but it ought to trigger Garson's fiery temper and make him confess inadvertently.

And if doing everything all legal-like didn't work, Slocum vowed Garson would never live to brag about how he murdered Curt Degraff.

The tracks he followed took him away from the fort, but clouds crossing the sky and a setting sliver of moon quickly stole any chance Slocum had of following the fresh prints. He got his bearings as the cloud layer broke and briefly showed the North Star, then he reluctantly laid out his bedroll and tried to sleep.

Slocum found himself thinking of Curt Degraff and the trails they had ridden together, then trying to piece together everything that happened outside the stables. The more he thought on it, the less he blamed Benjamin Washington. The only reason Garson had not fired again was the ruckus caused by the first shot, the one that had robbed Degraff of his life. Coming up with a reason for gunning down two men in the back would have been beyond Garson's ability to lie if he had gone ahead and shot Slocum, too.

Slocum knew one man to never turn his back to.

Somehow, this knowledge did not make him rest any easier. Finding Washington might be a real chore since the sergeant was savvy to the ways of hiding his tracks. He had to know as much as any Apache to catch the wily Indians, and Washington also had no reason to want Slocum to catch up with him. The expression on his face as Slocum took aim told of fear and distrust of any white man.

If he thought he was being accused of Degraff's murder, Washington was even more likely to hightail it and keep running—except that he had sneaked off the post, in violation of Garson's direct order. That meant he had some good reason to stay around Fort Selden. For a while.

Slocum had to find Washington, get him back to the major to tell what had happened and confirm Slocum's suspicions about Garson, then bury Degraff. It was a quick end for his partner and one that wasn't completely unexpected. Slocum just had not believed either of them would be cut down on an Army base.

Sleep began to work its fingers into his brain, but as he slipped away an ear-splitting shriek cut through the still night air, bringing him up with his six-shooter cocked and ready. He looked around as he tried to pinpoint the direction of the cry. His gelding jerked and tossed its head as it tried to get free of its tether.

Slocum slipped on his boots, shivered at the chilly night air and then began a slow circuit of his small camp. He stopped frequently and listened hard. The scream had not been followed with any more sound, but Slocum's sharp senses picked up the faint smell of burning piñon wood when he faced southward.

Others might be traveling and be camped for the night, but what prompted the scream? Slocum wasn't sure it had come from a man's throat either. It carried a higher pitch that might have been a woman in pain.

Placing one foot cautiously, testing to see if he stepped on anything that might crackle, and only then advancing, when he had solid ground under him, made for a painfully slow advance. If someone was in trouble, such caution might doom them. If Slocum didn't make sure his advance was shadow-quiet, it might mean both their lives.

For twenty minutes, he proceeded, the scent of firewood stronger than ever as he reached a six-foot-deep arroyo cut by spring runoffs. A thin thread of smoke twisted skyward, almost invisible until he reached the bank of the wash. Nestled on the sandy floor were a half dozen Apaches. One sat with his knees pulled up, but his head dropped occasionally as he drifted to sleep. In front of him burned embers from what had been a large fire.

Beyond the fire, away from the braves, sat a dark figure who silently struggled to pull free of a tether. Slocum watched a few minutes to be sure his eyes weren't playing tricks on him. They weren't. A white woman had been staked out and desperately tried to free herself. From the occasional bright flares of popping embers he saw how a rawhide band had been cruelly tied across her mouth to keep her quiet.

She had cried out for help, and Slocum was not going to abandon her. The only problem he had was how to rescue her from the middle of a war party.

He could shoot six times before all the Apaches were awake, but his chances of six killing or debilitating shots in the dark was nil. The guard dozed. That might let him sneak into the Indian camp and save the woman, but he couldn't count on it.

The low nicker of the Apaches' ponies gave him an idea. Slocum shoved his six-shooter into its holster and went to the small remuda a few yards up the arroyo. The Apaches had tied six horses to a rope stretched between the trunks of two sturdy mesquites. Slocum drew his knife and cut off a thorny branch a couple feet long, then worked on the end of the rope securing the horses.

He made a headstall of rope and then wove the prickly mesquite branch onto it. Slocum took a deep breath, then went to work. Everything had to be done fast, or he would find himself in a world of trouble. He quickly sliced the rope holding the horses, then threw the headstall around one horse's neck. He cinched it down so the thorns cut deep into the horse's neck.

He ducked back as the horse reared and kicked out instinctively at him. Then the horse lit out at a dead gallop. The other five followed in short order, not sure what was happening but willing to get away until they found out.

Slocum jumped up onto the arroyo bank and lay flat as the six Apaches rushed past, yelling curses at their fleeing horses. He had no time to waste. He rolled away from the bank, got to his feet and ran back to where the woman was still staked down.

The Indians were gone—for a few minutes. This was the only time Slocum was likely to get to save her.

"Keep quiet," he ordered. "We have to move fast if we're going to get out of here."

He tugged at the stake in the ground holding her and couldn't budge it. Slocum yanked out his knife again. The woman's eyes went wide at the sight, and she flinched back. With a savage whack, Slocum cut the rawhide cord holding her wrists. He took the time to sever the strand holding her hands together, then sliced through the bonds on her ankles.

"Umgh!" she grunted, trying to get the rawhide gag free.

"No time. They won't all go after the horses. Come on!" Slocum grabbed her wrist and felt blood oozing out. Her flesh was as cold as stone from having the circulation cut off so long. She got to her feet and stumbled. Her feet were as numb as her hands.

"Ur-ur," came the frantic noise. Slocum saw she couldn't walk easily. He sheathed his knife, bent and hoisted her over his shoulder. She wasn't heavy, but he staggered in the soft sand and went to one knee.

"Stop struggling," he warned her as he got his feet under him. Walking in the arroyo bottom was difficult but not as hard as enduring days of torture if the Apaches caught them. Slocum's legs kept pumping until he reached the embankment. With a powerful heave, he tossed her up onto the lip of the arroyo.

She rolled away. He quickly followed, saw what was happening behind them and grabbed her, pulling her to the ground.

The woman fought until she saw why he wanted to stay. Three Apaches had returned to the camp but had not seen that their prisoner had escaped.

The woman pressed close to Slocum. He felt her heart beating fiercely through her breast. She clutched his arm with surprising strength that told him she had regained circulation and could get away on her own. He took the time to work free the gagging piece of rawhide.

"Go on," he whispered in her ear. "I'll guard our back trail."

"No!" she said vehemently. "I'm not going out there alone. I heard them talking about all the snakes!"

Slocum almost laughed. The Apaches had a mortal fear

of rattlers and must have instilled some of that in their captive.

"You'd prefer a snakebite to what they'd do," he told her.

She shivered as if she had a fever. It took her several seconds and then she asked, "Where do I go?"

Slocum looked up and saw that the high, thin night clouds were drifting away. He pointed out the Pole Star.

"Can you follow that? Head straight toward it and don't try to dodge. That's the only way I'll ever find you."

"Where am I going, other than north?"

"My camp. Maybe a half mile off."

"I don't know," she said slowly. Then she faced him squarely and kissed him. "See you in your camp!" With that she was off, making more noise than Slocum would have liked but less than he expected from her after being tied up for so long.

He turned back to study the Apaches in the camp. They still had not noticed their captive was missing. All three huddled together near the dying fire, warming their hands and talking in low voices. As yet they were not interested in looking around to see if anything besides the escaped horses was amiss.

As he watched from the relative safety of the arroyo embankment, Slocum licked his lips where the woman had kissed him and tasted her blood. The rawhide strip had cut savagely into her flesh and left behind oozing wounds on her mouth. They reminded him anew of how vulnerable she was and how he had to come up with a plan of escape in a hurry if he wanted to get her the hell away from her Apache captors.

Slocum knew it was only a matter of time before the other three warriors caught their escaped ponies and brought them back to camp. They wouldn't have to be too bright to figure out someone had released and spooked the horses—and why.

Slocum considered his chances against the trio in camp and decided the factors against him before were still against him. They were alert, angry and armed now. While he stood a better chance against them, any gunfire would draw the remaining braves. With only the six rounds in his Colt, Slocum had no way of outgunning Apaches armed with rifles. He backed away slowly, hoping the woman had enough of a start toward his camp.

As he moved through the darkness, he made certain to place every step as carefully as when he had approached the Apache camp. Giving himself away now would only bring down a world of trouble on his head. After ten minutes, Slocum began to worry the woman had lost sight of the North Star or that she had gone some other way. After fifteen, he was sure she had gone astray in the dark. New clouds drifted across the sky, occasionally obscuring the Big Dipper and the North Star. And after more than twenty minutes, Slocum entered his camp.

His empty camp.

He had rescued the woman and then let her get disoriented and lose her way in the night.

5

Slocum wasted no time getting his bedroll stowed behind his saddle. As he swung the Western saddle up onto the back of his protesting gelding, Slocum heard movement from behind. He dropped the saddle, slapped leather, twisted into a crouch and took aim on . . . the woman he had rescued.

"That's a good way to get yourself killed, sneaking up on me like that," Slocum said, relaxing as he slid his six-shooter back, into his cross-draw holster.

"Sorry," she said, coming forward so he could get a good look at her for the first time. In spite of them being close before, close enough for her body to press into his, he had not taken the time to study her.

He liked what he saw. Under the grime, the scratches, and the concerned expression was a lovely face. Her brunette hair was filthy and tied back with a piece of twine, but looked as if it would fall down over her shoulders in a delightful cascade when clean and combed. Eyes like pools of chocolate stared at him, examining him as surely as he was studying her.

"How long have you been in camp?" Slocum asked.

"You're quick." she said with admiration. "Not many

men would have realized I was out there watching them." She moved a little closer so they touched again. "And you're mighty quick with that six-gun. Are you a gunman?"

"I was a scout out of Fort Selden," Slocum said, bending the truth a mite. He had never spent one minute as a scout working for the major, but he felt the need to make himself look better in her eyes than telling her he had been nothing more than a hunter.

"Was?"

"It's a long story, and we don't have much time." Slocum stooped, picked up his saddle and got it back on his horse. He spent the next few minutes cinching down the belly strap and making sure the saddle wouldn't come loose. With the Apaches likely to be on their trail anytime now, it might be a while before they could rest. He didn't want to stop to tend his tack with his—and the woman's—life on the line.

"I'm Caroline Thornton. The Apaches caught me while I was riding into town to get some supplies for my ma and pa."

"Your parents let you go alone? With the Apaches on the warpath?"

"We didn't know they were so near. All the reports we'd heard told of Victorio heading south into Mexico to stay with Juh."

"Victorio's got competition," Slocum explained, getting into the saddle. He kicked his foot free of the stirrup and reached down for Caroline. The woman hesitated, as if still not trusting him, then took his hand, got her foot in the stirrup and swung up behind him.

"What do you mean Victorio has competition?" she asked as they rode back in the direction of Fort Selden. Slocum figured they could reach the fort before sunup. He had not been on Washington's trail long enough to have gone more than fifteen miles.

"A brave named Dark Crow is intent on getting as big a war party together by leaving a trail of blood and death behind him."

"Dark Crow? Never heard of him," Caroline said. She gripped Slocum's belt and pulled herself closer. He was conscious of the way her breasts pressed into his back as she put her cheek against his shoulders. He said nothing and kept riding.

"Are you taking me home? It's not too far. At least I don't think so. The Apaches caught me two days ago, and we've been riding around ever since. I got turned around, so I don't know exactly where we are."

"Don't know where your pa's spread is so I'm taking you the one place I do know." He felt her stiffen again. Slocum added, "We're going to Fort Selden and ought to be there before sunrise."

"I can get home from the fort. It's a ways off, but I know the road."

"On foot?" he asked. "You don't have a horse."

"They killed my mare," Caroline said bitterly. "I was forced to ride in front of one of them. I had a time of it since they didn't have saddles. I—"

"Hush." Slocum reined back and listened hard.

"Riders," Caroline whispered. "Ahead of us."

"Between us and the fort," Slocum said. He listened harder, then jerked on the reins and got his gelding moving at a right angle to the direction they had been traveling. "We have to find a hiding place."

"They might be a patrol from the fort. In the dark, you can't tell."

"They're Apaches," Slocum said.

"How can you be so sure?"

"I listened. The sound of their horses' hooves against rock didn't sound like shod horses."

"And the Apache don't shoe their horses," she said. "I was right. You are quick on the uptake." A few seconds later she said, "You must have been one fine scout."

"Not so good," Slocum said. "I'm not getting away from the Apaches." The hoofbeats came closer, no matter how he turned.

"How did they get in front of us like that?" the brunette asked.

"Might be another party, a larger one. I hear at least ten horses."

"If they joined up, that would be a mighty strong fighting force." Caroline said. "This Dark Crow might be planning some truly horrible attack!"

"Probably," Slocum said, distracted. He cared less what Dark Crow planned than how to avoid the warriors. Rather than riding to the top of a sandy rise and silhouetting himself against the night sky, dark as it was, Slocum weaved in and out among clumps of prickly pears, occasional long whips of ocotillo and chest-high leafy creosote bushes. Fifteen minutes more riding brought him to a stand of cottonwoods, promising some water and a considerable amount of concealment. He dismounted and helped Caroline down.

"Why are we stopping here? It's so . . . exposed."

And it was. Slocum looked around for somewhere to hide and couldn't find it if the Indians rode among the trees. The only benefit came from being screened from a distance.

"I'll tether the horse a ways off. If the Apaches spot it, we'll have a few minutes warning when it whinnies." He led the gelding to the far side of the grove, such as it was, and tied the horse securely. He left the saddle on but took his bedroll, saddlebags and trusty Winchester. It wasn't much, but it might be enough if only one or two Indians found them.

He returned by a circuitous route to where he had left Caroline and was pleased when she spotted him immediately. She was alert and ready to fight.

"You scared me," she said. "Why'd you sneak around instead of coming straight back?"

"Just scouting," he lied.

"You were testing me," she said accusingly.

"You're mighty quick on the uptake, too," he said, smiling.

This brought a real smile to her lips. Slocum reached out and touched them. She winced and then caught herself.

"Sorry. That hurts."

Slocum remembered the kiss she had given him back where he had rescued her. Caroline was immensely attractive, in spite of her disheveled appearance. Slocum's green eyes bored into her softer brown ones and silent communication flowed.

He bent to kiss her gently. The world seemed to slow and then stop around them as the kiss deepened into something more than a simple kiss. Her fingers began roving his body, caressing, touching, teasing. When she reached his gun belt, she began fumbling with the buckle.

"You're overdressed," she said.

"For what?"

"For what I have in mind—and for what you want to do, too."

As she freed it, Slocum caught his gun belt rather than let it drop to the ground. But as he held the belt with its heavy six-shooter, the brunette worked furiously at the buttons on his jeans.

"My, my, look at that," she said with some satisfaction. Caroline looked up at him with sparkling eyes, then began stroking up and down his hard length. As she gripped down firmly, it began pulsing with powerful need. "I hope you're not quick in all things."

Before he could answer, she dived forward like a hunting hawk. Her cut lips circled the purpled tip of his shaft and fastened down solidly. She began licking and kissing

the fleshy length until Slocum turned weak in the knees.
He sank down, somehow getting the bedroll spread out
beneath them.

They collapsed in a heap on the blanket, arms wrapped
around one another. Slocum stroked over the woman's
face, her cheek, jaw, lower. His hand found a delightfully
warm mound of flesh when he worked down to her chest.
Caroline sighed softly and then unbuttoned her blouse so
her bare breasts spilled out for Slocum's delectation.

He dived down between Caroline's pillowy mounds,
licking and kissing as she had done on his manhood.
Tongue licking feverishly, he worked his way to the top
of one snowy crest and found the nipple capping it. He
sucked the throbbingly hard nub between his lips and then
used both teeth and tongue on it. He coasted down Caroline's right breast and worked his way wetly up her left.
When he duplicated the treatment he had already given
her right nipple, he felt her heart beating furiously.

"I . . . I feel like I'm on fire, John," she sobbed out. Her
fingers raked through his lank dark hair and kept his head
firmly down on her luscious breasts. Slocum was content
to sample the feast before him. He felt the woman begin
to twitch and jerk as her body responded to his oral attack.

He enjoyed this, but the urges within his loins were
mounting to the point that he did not know if he could
restrain himself. Slocum pulled free and worked lower,
his tongue leaving wet tracks down her bare belly until
he reached the fleecy triangle hidden between her thighs.

Tasting her oily inner juices as he licked across her
nether lips told him she was as ready as he was. Slocum
hurriedly worked his way back up and positioned himself
between her wantonly spread legs.

"Yes, John, now. I need you so. Oh!" She gasped as
he found the target and slammed forward. There was nothing slow and easy about his entry. He wanted the lovely

brunette. Her response told him she wanted him as much, if not more.

She lifted her rump off the ground and tried to grind her crotch into his in a vain effort to take even more of his steely hard shaft into her steamy interior. Caroline reached out and gripped his upper arms. She pulled herself up so she could kiss him hard on the mouth. Slocum tasted blood again, mingled with the woman's juices.

This drove him on. His hips took on a life of their own, moving faster and faster. He sank balls-deep into her molten core and then moved in small circles, stirring her lust even more. Caroline fell back flat and returned the favor.

Slocum gasped when it felt as if she had crushed his hidden length with her strong inner muscles. Pulling out and driving back into her hungering body was harder—and infinitely more exciting. A lewd sucking sound echoed through the small grove as she overflowed every time he filled her. They both gasped and moaned as he continued to drive like a locomotive piston. And then the woman's lush body trembled and shook until she vented a loud cry of sheer ecstasy.

Slocum bent down and stifled the cry of joy with another kiss, but his hips never slowed as they rammed forward. He felt the fire deep within his loins begin to spread outward. He moved faster, the friction of their passion-racked bodies finally igniting his release. He exploded like a volcano. Slocum was distantly aware of Caroline again crying out as new waves of rapture overwhelmed her.

He sank down on her supine body, his chest mashing flat her breasts. They lay face to face. Slocum kissed her again, but this time there was no blood.

"Does your mouth hurt?" he asked.

"How can it when I'm feeling so good everywhere else?" Caroline asked, smiling. She craned her neck slightly and kissed him firmly. Slocum was in no hurry to move but did eventually and stretched out beside her.

The soft night wind blew over their naked flesh, chilling them. Slocum pulled up the blanket and moved closer to her.

"I ought to rescue women from the Apaches more often," Slocum said.

"Do you consider this your due?" she asked somewhat sternly.

"No, but it surely was nice," Slocum said as he kissed her again.

Caroline broke off and said, "It was nice, and you can rescue me whenever you want. Be sure to bring this, though." Her roving hand found his limp organ and began massaging it. Before he knew it, he was stiff again. And several more times throughout the night.

"Don't get me wrong, John, I don't mind spending time with you, but I'm getting mighty tired of running from shadows."

Slocum agreed, but to him they weren't mere shadows. They were Apache braves intent on lifting their scalps. For two days he had dodged the war parties as he tried to get back to Fort Selden. The entire countryside swarmed with the Apaches, however, and he had ridden farther from the fort rather than to it.

"The nights aren't so bad," he said.

"It's not the same when you're distracted by every little sound," Caroline complained.

"Any of those sounds might be an Apache sneaking up on us."

"Not all of them, though," she said, wrapping her arms tighter around his chest and pressing against his back. Slocum tried to turn in the saddle to see her but couldn't. She rested her cheek against his shoulders as she had the first night when he had rescued her.

Looking around, Slocum saw only the usual desert sights with shimmering curtains of heat dancing on the horizon. He considered angling back toward the fort again but knew of at least one band of Apaches raiding nearby. He had hoped to find a patrol, even one led by Lieutenant Garson, but activity out of the fort had been curiously quiet. He had to believe they were hunkering down as they waited for Dark Crow to attack them.

He changed his mind about where to find safety.

"How do I find your pa's spread?" he asked.

"You're taking me home instead of to the fort?" Caroline asked. Her tone lightened at the prospect of seeing her people again.

"Major Cavendish probably has his hands full dealing with Dark Crow. That might be enough diversion to get you home."

"It'll be so good being with my folks," she said wistfully. Then Caroline straightened, reached over Slocum's shoulder and pointed east in the direction of three lumpy hills. "That way. My father's ranch is butted up against the base of the center mountain."

Slocum estimated three more days on the trail, if they avoided Dark Crow. It turned out to be four when they had to skirt a large Apache encampment.

Never was Slocum happier to see a ranch than when Caroline yelped with glee and pointed to her family's ranch house sitting near the slope of the middle mountain she had pointed out days earlier.

"There, John, that's it. When can we get there?"

"Not long," he said. He was tired from the trail, and his horse was exhausted carrying twice the weight. Riding full gallop for the house was appealing but would cause his gelding to collapse under them. He urged the horse down into the range land surrounding the house, to a narrow double-rutted road and then toward this outpost of civilization.

"It'll be so good seeing them again," Caroline said. "Not that I've minded the past week or so. I never thought being kidnapped by Indians would turn out so well. But they're my kin, and they don't know what happened to me."

Slocum had no reason to reply. He let Caroline ramble on as she got more excited at seeing her parents and telling them the good news that she was safe. Slocum started to worry a mite when no one came out onto the broad front porch to greet them. He looked around the yard but did not dismount.

"Wait," he said, stopping Caroline from jumping down.

"What's wrong? I want to find my folks!"

"Why didn't somebody see us coming and greet us? Where is everyone?"

"Why, they might be out," Caroline said, beginning to worry.

"How many hands does your pa have working here?"

"A dozen or so. They come and go so fast, it's hard to know at any given time."

"I don't see a trace of anyone," Slocum said, reaching over and slipping the leather thong off his six-shooter. "You stay mounted and let me go scout a bit."

He got his leg over the saddle horn and dropped to the ground. His tired muscles protested a moment, then he got the kinks worked out of his legs as he climbed the four steps to the front porch. Listening hard for any human sound, he went to the door and rapped.

Nothing.

He turned and put his finger to his lips, cautioning Caroline to stay quiet. Slocum motioned that he was going around to the side. She nodded but her eyes darted to the other side of the house, making Slocum believe there might be something untoward there. He reversed his course to see what Caroline was staring at.

"No, John, wait!" she called.

Slocum jumped the railing at the end of the porch and hit the ground in a crouch. Caroline had spotted Benjamin

Washington peeking around the house but was not going
to alert Slocum.

Washington's hand flashed to his six-gun, then froze
when he saw what he faced. Slocum had the Colt Navy
out, cocked 'and aimed squarely at the deserter's belly.

"Don't go for that gun," Slocum warned. Washington
had started again for the six-shooter tucked into his broad
leather cavalry belt, as if thinking Slocum might not pull
the trigger. He still wore his uniform shirt but the stripes
had been ripped off.

"You're not takin' me back to the fort."

Slocum stood, keeping the gun leveled. Before he could
explain that he wanted Washington's testimony to corrob-
orate his own against Garson, Slocum heard footsteps
coming up behind him.

"Caroline?" he asked. A whistling sound warned him
of danger, but it was too late. The heavy board struck him
on the back of the head and knocked him facedown into
the dirt. His six-shooter went flying, but he tried to scram-
ble after it.

He looked up to see Caroline holding his Colt in both
hands.

"Don't make me shoot you, John," she said. The grim
look on her face and the determination in her brown eyes
convinced him she would cut him down if he moved a
muscle.

6

"I won't shoot unless you force me, John." From the steady grip and the set to the woman's jaw, Slocum believed her. He held up his hands and wondered where Washington had gone. When he heard the hoofbeats quickly fading into the distance, he knew. Benjamin Washington had been hiding out here and now hightailed it into the mountains where tracking him would be a chore.

"Why are you doing this?" Slocum asked. "Washington's a deserter." He held back telling her why he wanted Washington to return to Fort Selden with him. It would only cloud the issue and might make her think he was spinning a tall tale.

"He has his reasons," she said.

"How do you know? You were being held captive by the Apaches when he lit out."

"He . . . he's told me how the lieutenant treats him. I take it as a measure of his confidence in me and my folks that Benjamin came here to hide."

"Where are your folks? All the hands?"

"You can't think Benjamin killed them?" Caroline's scorn for such an idea carried strongly. Slocum had to agree with her on this score. No matter how desperate the deserter might be, he could never kill or run off all the ranch hands and the owner of such a large spread.

"I need to get him back to the fort," Slocum said.

"Well, you won't," Caroline said firmly.

For a long minute neither said anything. Then Slocum slowly lowered his hands.

"Will you shoot me or do you want my arms to fall off?"

"I don't want to shoot you at all, John. I just don't want you turning Benjamin over to that terrible Lieutenant Garson. Or Lieutenant Porter. He's almost as bad."

"The major commands Fort Selden and seems honest enough. It wouldn't be Garson's call what happens to the sergeant."

Caroline looked over her shoulder, then lowered the heavy gun. Slocum made no move to take it from her. She studied him for a moment, then said, "Aren't you going to take your pistol back? It's mighty heavy."

He went to her and silently took it. After he gently lowered the hammer, he thrust it back into his holster. Slocum took a deep breath and walked past Caroline, looking into the hills behind the ranch house. Going after Washington would be a fool's errand. The rocky ground would make tracking hard, and with his horse all worn out from carrying two people for almost a week it would never keep up with Washington.

"Do you know where he's headed? He had the look of a man with a destination in mind."

"You flushed him," Caroline said. "He probably hid out here and you ran him off."

Slocum looked around the deserted ranch, wondering what had happened. He left Caroline behind as he went to the barn and looked inside. All the animals were gone. The corral behind the barn was similarly empty. The bunkhouse hadn't been used for a few days, but most of the cowboys' belongings were properly stowed, as if they had just ridden out for a day or two of rounding up strays.

He went back to the house and joined Caroline inside.

"Any trace of your parents?" he asked.

"They left a note," Caroline said, clutching a scrap of paper. "Mama worried about the Apaches attacking, so Papa took her into Mineral Springs. They figured she'd be safer there with all the others in town."

"Why not take her to Fort Selden?"

Caroline looked as if she had bitten into a bitter persimmon. "I've heard Benjamin's stories of how Lieutenant Garson acts. No one is safe there. Better to stay with civilians than be under that devil in blue's thumb."

Slocum shrugged it off.

"What about the cowboys? Did they just up and leave?"

"I'm not sure about them, but I think Papa had them out on the range protecting the herd from the Apaches. We can't afford to lose many more head. This has been a good year but last was a terrible drought that cost us most of the herd."

"You have to recoup," Slocum said, knowing the boom and bust of ranching well. He sank onto a sofa and felt as if the weight of the world descended on his shoulders.

"What are you thinking, John?" she asked.

"I have to take Washington back to the fort," he said. "It's for the best."

"I doubt it," she said. Then Caroline's shoulders squared. "Will you promise me you won't let Garson kill Benjamin?"

"Yes," he said simply. Slocum saw no reason to embellish it with fancy promises.

"Very well," she said, sitting next to him on the sofa. "I believe you will keep Benjamin from being murdered. It's no good if he is on the run for the rest of his life. It's not the kind of man he is."

Slocum turned a little and looked at her. A thousand

thoughts jumbled in his head, but only one bobbed to the top.

"There's no sense riding out on a tired horse. And we need rest, too."

"Food first," Caroline said, smiling. "Then bed." Her smile turned to a wicked grin. "*Then* rest."

"Are you sure he'd come this way?" Slocum asked skeptically. They rode away from the mountains where Washington would be almost impossible to track and toward the far side of the bowl holding the Thornton spread. "We're going toward Fort Selden."

"Keep an eye out for Indians," she said from behind him. "He won't just leave New Mexico Territory. Not without Maybelle."

"Who's that? His sweetheart?"

"His wife," Caroline said. "Not many of the buffalo soldiers have wives. And the ones who do leave them somewhere more civilized. Benjamin is luckier because Maybelle wanted to go along with him, no matter how hard it was."

"Is that part of his problem with Garson?" Slocum asked. Enlisted men weren't supposed to have wives accompanying them to outposts like Fort Selden. A few officers brought wives, but usually only those of the highest rank. Slocum had not noticed any women around Fort Selden, but then he had not been there very long.

"I can't say, but Benjamin and Garson never hit it off well. From the first day, the lieutenant found fault with everything Benjamin did."

"He still shouldn't have deserted," Slocum said. If Washington had stayed and testified against Garson, the lieutenant might be in the fort stockade waiting for a firing squad now.

Or perhaps not. Slocum realized officers were scarce on the frontier, especially at posts garrisoned by buffalo soldiers. Nothing might have happened to Garson.

"Garson would never let Benjamin have leave, so he took to sneaking out to see Maybelle. How can you blame a man for wanting to see his wife?" Caroline sounded plaintive.

"I can't, but he disobeyed orders," Slocum said, remembering his days in the CSA. "Orders have to be followed or men die. What if Dark Crow attacked while Washington was off seeing Maybelle? His absence could have spelled the deaths of many of his men."

"If, if, if," scoffed Caroline. "That never happened, did it? Benjamin is very conscientious."

"How do you know him so well? He lit out while you were held captive. You can't know the details of why he deserted." The more Slocum talked, the more he came to sympathize with Washington.

"We get our supplies in Mineral Springs. Mother and Maybelle got to be good friends. One thing led to another and, well, sometimes we arranged for Maybelle and Benjamin to get together on one pretext or another."

"You mean your pa would ask for a patrol—headed by Washington—to check his spread? Then Maybelle and Washington would meet while the rest of the patrol went on a wild-goose chase?"

"Something like that," Caroline said contritely. "I know it was dangerous. What if the Apaches attacked somewhere else while Benjamin was with his wife? But it never happened, and Garson was always so irrational and cruel."

"Garson is all that and more," Slocum said, remembering vividly Degraff's last seconds of life, how he looked, the reason he had died.

He turned his attention to the terrain and the chance for running across a roving band of Apaches. Twice Slocum diverted from the road to circle and come back miles away because he feared ambushes. He was not certain he had to be so careful, but taking unnecessary chances with his and Caroline's lives didn't strike him as prudent.

"Is that Mineral Springs?" Slocum asked as they neared a pitiful collection of adobe houses. He thought it was. How many mud brick towns could there be in the middle of nowhere? By his reckoning, they were only a few miles from Fort Selden, but he had never been here before.

"Yes," Caroline said with some distaste. "This isn't the best section of town. Those are whorehouses for the soldiers."

"Where's the better section of town?" Slocum asked, amused at her aversion to what existed near every fort in the West.

"Keep on riding. You'll get there in a quarter mile or so." Caroline rode with her eyes straight ahead, refusing to take notice of the scantily clad women peeking out of doorways. Some of the bolder whores waved and called to Slocum. He politely tipped his hat in their direction, ignored both the come-ons and the insults about his manhood as he passed by, then got to a tight collection of stores and houses.

"Maybelle's staying with Miz Perkins. She runs about the only decent boardinghouse in town."

"I can believe that," Slocum said. If Mineral Springs had a population of a hundred, it would surprise him. And at least ten of that number were back down the road in the cribs.

He pulled his hat down to shade his eyes. The sun sank fast and plunged the town into darkness. Unlike many towns, Mineral Springs had no gas lights. All lighting was done by fireplace or candle. Slocum licked his lips and looked behind him, trying to find the saloon. He had somehow missed it on his way through town and couldn't locate it now, not that he would enter such an establishment while Caroline rode with him.

But it had been a powerful long time since whiskey had

wetted his lips, and the trail had been dusty and dry.

"There, that house," Caroline said, pointing to an adobe that looked exactly like the others around it. Slocum reined in and dismounted, helped Caroline to the ground and then tethered his tired gelding before going to the front door. By the time he got there, Caroline was already talking to a tired-looking woman with her hair drawn back in a severe bun.

"Miz Perkins," Slocum greeted. The woman's eyes widened slightly.

"How do you know my name? I've never met you before. I'd've remembered."

"I spoke of you," Caroline said hastily.

"What's he want with Maybelle? I won't let any of them bluecoats take her away. She's the best maid I ever had."

"We only want to talk to her, Miz Perkins," explained Caroline. Slocum thought it best to let the woman do the talking. Even so, it took Caroline several more minutes before the landlady vanished into the dark interior. He heard her shouting for Maybelle. A full minute passed before a slight chocolate-skinned woman came out, looking like a rabbit ready to run from a coyote. She relaxed a little seeing Caroline but kept darting furtive glances in Slocum's direction.

"Miss Thornton," Maybelle said. "I didn't 'spect to see you anytime soon."

"Let's talk," Caroline said, guiding Maybelle to one of a pair of chairs near the adobe's front door. The two women sat while Slocum remained standing.

"This is about Benjamin, isn't it?" Maybelle looked more scared than ever.

"I want to escort him back to the fort, ma'am," Slocum said. "He shouldn't have deserted, but I—" He stopped when he saw the woman's horrified expression. "You didn't know your husband had left the fort without permission?"

"Why, no," Maybelle said, startled at this news, and Slocum believed her. He glared at Caroline. The woman had led him on a wild-goose chase to give Washington added time to escape. Slocum's gut feeling that the deserter had gone into the mountains behind the Thornton ranch house was probably correct, and Caroline had caused him to dally and then ride a full day in the opposite direction.

By now Washington might be a hundred miles away.

"It's important that I escort him back to Fort Selden," Slocum said gently.

"He deserted?" Maybelle's shocked expression turned to tears. "You won't hurt him none, will you, mister?" She looked at the worn ebony butt of his Colt, the way he wore the holster, the way he stood and moved. Maybelle had jumped to the conclusion Slocum was a bounty hunter sent out after her husband.

"I won't," Slocum said sincerely. "It's a long story but I need him alive to back up charges against Lieutenant Garson."

"You ain't lyin'?"

"Mr. Slocum is a truthful man," Caroline said, eyeing him. He read her expression perfectly. If he lied about bringing Washington back alive, he would have to answer to her.

Slocum would rather have all Dark Crow's warriors after him than an angry Caroline Thornton.

"Have you seen your husband recently, Mrs. Washington?"

"I, no, I haven't seen Benjamin in so long. He sneaked out like he always does to come see me, but that was a week back. I heard the town folks talkin' 'bout them Indians bein' ever'where. Benjamin was always good 'bout fightin' and trackin' Apaches, and I reckoned he was on patrol. Sometimes he's gone for weeks. Gets powerful lonesome without my Benjamin."

"Where might he go, if he didn't come to see you?" asked Slocum.

Maybelle shook her head, silently showing she had no idea. Again Slocum believed her.

"Benjamin knows the badlands as good as anyone," Caroline said. "If he wanted to hide out for a week or two, nobody could find him there. Nobody."

"That's true," Maybelle said. "He patrolled out there with his company so much, he knows the land like his own hand."

"And the badlands are on the other side of the mountains to the east of your ranch," Slocum said.

Caroline smiled weakly and shrugged, as if saying, *I only did what I thought was right.*

"You stay with Mrs. Washington," Slocum told Caroline. "It's too dangerous being alone out at your ranch."

"Your mama's here in town, too," Maybelle spoke up. "She's over at the Zamora place." Maybelle looked up to Slocum and explained, "Mr. Zamora owns the general store, and he and his fam'ly have a house right behind."

"John," said Caroline, getting to her feet. She grabbed his hand and held it tightly. "You won't—"

"I won't hurt him," he said. "Believe me, I need him alive and able to testify."

"But he's a deserter, isn't he?" asked Maybelle. "That means he broke the law."

"Major Cavendish hasn't heard all the facts yet. He won't be as inclined to court-martial your husband when he hears what we both have to say."

Caroline looked at him curiously. Before she could ask, Slocum pulled free.

He tipped his hat in the women's direction, mounted and rode back the way he had come, heading into the

distant mountains so he could get into the badlands beyond. Slocum hoped Washington wasn't as good a frontiersman as the women claimed. If he was, he would never
track down the cavalry trooper.

7

Slocum could not remember the sun ever being hotter or brighter. He mopped at his forehead with his bandanna, then tied the wet cloth back around his neck. Sampling a bit of water from his canteen did little to take away the razor-sharp edge of thirst, since he had been in the badlands to the east of the Rio Grande for two days on Benjamin Washington's trail and had found very little drinkable water.

He studied the sunbaked ground and thought he saw a faint trace of Washington's horse. Slocum dismounted and knelt, studying the imprint closely. With the fitful wind blowing over the desert, he might be imagining a trail where none existed, yet he had come directly over the mountains behind the Thornton spread and into this hellhole. Once or twice he had seen fresh spoor that must belong to Washington. But after those clues he had been riding on instinct alone.

More than once Slocum had stopped to rest and reconsider his chase. Taking Washington back would mean two of them could testify against Garson, but would that be enough to convict? Slocum wondered if he might not be better off calling out the lieutenant and gunning him down. He was certain Garson had murdered Degraff only because he had missed a chance to shoot Slocum in the back. Either crime deserved hanging, but the cavalry officer was not likely to stand trial with testimony of only one man.

But would Cavendish listen to a busted-to-the-ranks sergeant who had deserted? Slocum did not know. For his two cents, Benjamin Washington was a better soldier than Garson could ever hope to be. The sergeant had rescued him and Degraff from Dark Crow's warriors and had shown courage and skill fighting the Apaches. Garson had shown neither of those traits and had lapsed to backshooting when it came down to settling a feud.

Degraff just had the bad luck to be in the wrong place and had taken a bullet meant for Slocum.

Slocum stood and stared into the heat-curtained distance. The land was dry and rocky, with occasional clumps of tough, thorny mesquite and the dull green greasewood. Very little else grew here. Shielding his eyes against the sun, Slocum scanned the horizon the best he could for any hint of movement. If Washington was out there, he failed to see him.

Rather than mounting, Slocum walked a spell, with his horse following dutifully. He did not want to tire out the gelding here in the middle of such blistering land. If there had been even a hint of shade, Slocum would have gladly curled up in it and rested until closer to sundown. But save for the few square feet of restlessly moving shade cast by the low-growing bushes, the land was sunbaked and impossibly hot.

As he made his way, Slocum's mind began to wander. He thought of Caroline Thornton and the days they had spent together—and the nights. She was one fine woman, and he would gladly rescue her again. He could almost see her ahead of him, beckoning him on.

"Hurry, John," the brunette beauty said, her hand reaching out to him. "Come on. This way, this way."

"Caroline? What are you doing here?" His cracked lips barely formed the words. He took more of his water, but it did nothing to sate his real thirst. When Slocum looked back, Caroline was gone. He hunted for her amid the scattered clumps of prickly pear and creosote bush, but she had vanished.

Where'd you go? he wondered. He looked down at his feet for some sign and took a quick step back. Slocum dropped to his knees in the hot sand and found horse manure only a day or two old. "Washington!"

Caroline had led him to the deserter's trail. But where was she? How had she gotten in front of him to beckon him on? Slocum swung into the saddle and got his tired horse moving in the direction Washington had taken days earlier.

Or maybe it was less. Slocum tried to focus on the condition of the manure. Was it dry enough to have been there for days or only hours? The sun could bake anything quickly. But Washington would not travel in such heat. He would go to ground. That meant the trace had been left before sunrise. Or was it later?

Slocum's head began spinning, and he clutched hard at his saddle horn to keep from falling off. He shook himself, realizing the heat had robbed him of his senses. Even as this fact meandered down into his consciousness, his horse reared, forcing Slocum to fight even to hang on. The gelding twisted and went sunfishing, almost throwing Slocum. He clung to the reins and tried to subdue the bucking bronco.

He regained a measure of control, but the horse bolted and raced across the uneven ground.

"Whoa, slow down!" Slocum cried. And then he was sailing through the air and as suddenly landing hard on his back. The air blasted from his lungs, and he felt steel bands tighten around his chest as the sun burned his face.

Slocum gasped and then gagged before rolling to his side. He curled up and panted until he got his wind back. Getting to shaky feet, he went back to where his horse had stepped into a deep hole.

The horse whinnied piteously and fought to get back onto its feet. Slocum tried to calm it, saw the extent of the damage done to its leg and drew his six-shooter. A single shot ended the horse's agony. With smoking six-gun in hand, Slocum sat heavily on the hot ground and just stared. He wasn't thinking clearly, but he knew his chance of capturing Benjamin Washington had just died.

If he wasn't damned lucky, he would die out in the badlands, too.

Slinging his saddlebags over one shoulder and the almost empty canteen over the other, Slocum got moving. He had to get out of the sun. He had to put miles behind him to find water or shade. One foot lifted and then fell heavily before he willed the other to repeat the action. Slocum kept moving like this for some time until he realized he had no idea what direction he was headed.

"Into the badlands," he moaned when he got to the top of a sandy rise and looked around. "I've been walking *into* the desert, not out of it." For no good reason, he found this funny and laughed until his sides hurt.

Slocum got his emotions under control and knew what had to be done. He turned and found the three lumpy mountains far to the west promising sanctuary from the heat and perhaps even a taste of sweet water. If he could reach those distant mountains, he could get to the Thornton spread on the other side.

He would be safe then. Safe. Slocum started walking.

Under the sun. Without any more water. Staggering as life was burned from his dehydrated body.

He fell to his knees and saw a patch of shade ahead. Refusing to give up and die, he crawled on hands and knees for the shade, only to find it was hardly enough to shelter him. Strangely, the shadow was long and wide and man-shaped.

As his head slipped into the shade, Slocum twisted so he could look up. The sun burned away any details of the man standing over him. But Slocum knew.

"Washington," he said in a cracked voice. Then he passed out.

Slocum awoke, thrashing about. He had a terrible nightmare of drowning. In the hot desert he was drowning. From a distance came a booming voice.

"Stop fightin' me."

Benjamin Washington. It had to be the deserter's voice he heard in his nightmare. Slocum rolled to one side and tried to sit up, only to find himself pinned down. Water sloshed into his mouth, gagging him.

"Water?"

"This is about the best watering hole east of Fort Selden," Washington said.

Slocum blinked his eyes clear of water and saw the man towering above him. He tried to piece everything together but couldn't.

"I found you," Washington supplied. "Couldn't let you die so I brought you here."

"Water," Slocum said, wiping his face. He rolled back onto his belly and thrust his face into the pool, sucking in water greedily. When he got his fill, he turned over and sat up. He felt the weight of his Colt Navy still in its holster. From the way the sun shone on Washington's blue uniform sleeves Slocum saw where the sergeant's stripes had been sewed and then torn off when the man was demoted.

"What are you going to do?" asked Washington. He stood at ease, but nearby lay a rifle, and he had a six-shooter thrust into his belt.

"We've got to go back to the fort," Slocum said. Washington tensed.

"They'll hang me for deserting."

"You have to back up my accusation," Slocum said. "Garson shot my partner in the back. I suspect Garson was trying to gun me down and missed, but Degraff's still dead at his hand."

"You aren't out after a bounty on my head?" Washington ran his hand through his tightly coiled hair.

"You wouldn't have run if Garson hadn't gunned down Degraff, would you?" Slocum asked.

Washington shook his head sadly. "You got that wrong, Mistah Slocum. I was on my way off the post when you and your friend heard me. I was deserting."

"I don't want to hear that." Slocum said. "Garson's a backshooter and has to be called out on it."

"He's more than that, a whale of a lot more than that," Washington said resentfully.

"What your reasons for leaving Fort Selden are don't interest me. All that I care about is seeing Garson brought to justice."

"If I don't go?"

"You'll be leaving a mighty fine wife behind," Slocum said, playing his trump card. "If you're on the run from the cavalry, you'll never be able to see Maybelle again."

"Garson made it danged hard to see her when I was in the Army," Washington said. "Don't see how deserting makes it any worse."

"It will," Slocum said. Washington worked over the troubles facing him. Slocum let him mull them a spell, then asked, "Why did you save me? I was a goner, out of my head with heat. I never noticed it creeping up on me."

"That happens," Washington said, thankful to be talking on a less difficult subject. "I always tell my troopers to ride in threes. Sometimes, two won't know they need water or rest but the third will."

"I suspect you don't lose many patrols."

"Not many," Washington said, a smile splitting his face.

"If you wanted to leave, I couldn't stop you," Slocum said.

"Reckon you got it right about what I want to do," Washington said. "Not seein' Maybelle is bad, but my men would get in a world of trouble running down Dark Crow and his braves. Hate to see any of them scalped."

Slocum got to his feet, his wet shirt drying almost immediately in the hot, dry desert air. He looked around and wondered how far he had been from this small oasis in the desert. He didn't think he had been unconscious long, but Washington had brought him here and given him water. Benjamin Washington had saved his life when he thought Slocum was intent on nothing but taking him in, dead or alive.

"You aren't funnin' me on bringing charges against Garson, are you?"

Slocum didn't have to answer. The expression on his face was answer enough. The buffalo soldier nodded once, tossed Slocum his canteen to fill and pointed to a sway-backed horse tethered a few yards back.

"That's how we get back. Since she's not likely to hold both our weight, one of us has to walk."

"I've done worse in my day," Slocum said, sloshing the water around the mouth of his canteen to get rid of grit.

"Might be we can take turns riding," Washington amended. "We can stay here for another couple hours, then it'll be cool enough to go home."

They had crossed the mountains and gotten to the Thornton spread by the second day. Slocum was foot sore and tired but still game to keep going. The notion Garson was going to be seeing the world from the other side of iron bars kept him going. But the Thornton ranch house was still deserted, worrying Slocum. When he mentioned his concern to Washington, the brawny buffalo soldier shrugged it off.

"Dark Crow has everyone stirred up. I can see Mistah Thornton keeping his entire crew out to save what cattle they can."

"Why not round them up and bring the herd closer to the house?" asked Slocum.

"Might be what he's doing. His herd's scattered over three or four sections of rangeland. Even with the wet spring, grazing's hard out here."

Slocum wished he could have begged a mount from the rancher, but the barn was as empty now as when he had been here before with Caroline. He kept slogging along on his way back to Fort Selden. It took another day to get to the cavalry post.

The two guards at the gate stepped out and stared. Slocum took it as a good sign neither of the soldiers leveled their rifles at Washington.

"Is the major in his office?" Slocum asked. If Cavendish was out on patrol or called away for another meeting, Slocum intended to lay low with Washington until the post commander returned. Turning Washington over to Garson was a certain death sentence.

"Surely is, Mr. Slocum. Hey, Sarge, is he bringin' you in or are you bringin' him in?" The sentry grinned.

"A little of both, maybe," Washington allowed. "There any problem with H Company?"

"Nuthin' you can't whip, Sarge."

"I'm not a sergeant anymore," Washington said.

"We'll see about that, too," Slocum promised. He asked the guard, "Can we go right to the major?"

"I'll be happy to escort you, suh," the guard said. "Wouldn't want the lieutenant gettin' his dander up, would we?"

Slocum and Washington made their way directly across the parade ground straight to the major's office. Slocum put his hand on the butt of his six-shooter when he saw another lieutenant, Porter, stick his head out of the officers quarters. When Porter spotted them, he ducked back. Slocum knew he and Garson were thicker than thieves, and it was only a matter of minutes before the diminutive lieutenant came boiling out, blood in his eye.

Slocum herded Washington into Cavendish's office. The major looked up, startled. His mouth opened, then closed like a beached fish.

"Major, we got some serious talking to do about the situation."

"A moment, Mr. Slocum. I'll see you get the reward for returning this deserter to our post."

Washington stiffened and looked angrily at Slocum. Slocum pushed Washington to one side and kicked the door shut behind him when he saw Garson hurrying in the direction of the office.

"Listen up, Major. There are serious matters to be talked out."

Garson began banging on the door, demanding to be let in.

"Garson tried to kill me," Slocum said coldly. "He missed me and shot Degraff. Washington saw it." Slocum gave the buffalo soldier a hard look, cautioning him to silence. Washington had not seen the crime but had come on the scene a few seconds later. "Garson wants to silence both Washington and me to hide his crime."

"Why'd he want to kill you? Or Degraff?" Cavendish frowned at the noise Garson made banging on the door.

"That's something to come out at a trial," Slocum said. "But Washington didn't shoot Degraff. You have my word on that. And he was afraid of what Garson would do because he saw who pulled the trigger. That's why he lit out the way he did."

Major Cavendish turned angrily toward the closed door and shouted, "Stop that pounding, Lieutenant, or I'll hang your ears on the flagpole!" The officer took a deep breath and turned his attention back to Slocum and Washington.

"That's a mighty serious charge to levy against an officer."

"I'm making it, and I'll swear to at a court-martial," Slocum said.

"Sergeant," Cavendish said. He caught himself. "Private Washington, is what he said true?"

"No, sir, it is not," Washington said. "I was on my way off the post. I was deserting when the shooting happened."

"You're confessing to desertion?" This took Cavendish aback.

"I didn't shoot Degraff. I reckon everything Mr. Slocum says about the killing is true, but Garson didn't chase me off."

"No, I suspect not." Cavendish looked from Slocum to Washington and back. Then he bellowed, "Lieutenant Garson, you may enter now!"

Garson rushed in, looking around wildly. He had his pistol out but couldn't figure out who to point it at first.

"Put your weapon away, Lieutenant," Cavendish ordered.

"They're killers, sir. Both of them."

"Lieutenant!" Cavendish barked. The small officer took a step back and reluctantly lowered his six-shooter but did not holster it. Slocum considered what might happen to him if he threw down on Garson and shot him where he stood. It would be fairer than the way he had backshot Degraff, but Slocum doubted the major would see it that way.

"Serious charges have been brought against you, Lieutenant. I am not inclined to believe them, but an investigation should be conducted. You are relieved of your command until further notice."

"What?" Garson looked stunned at this. "But he's a

deserter and I'm not so sure Slocum didn't shoot his own partner!"

"There's no evidence Mr. Slocum did any such thing. As to Private Washington, he has confessed to desertion and will be put into the stockade until all evidence has been presented."

"Garson ought to be locked up, not Washington," Slocum said.

"You have made your opinion apparent, Mr. Slocum. *This* is the way it will be. Guard! Take Private Washington to the stockade and place him under round-the-clock guard. At least two armed soldiers at all times."

The guard who had escorted them from the gate looked startled, then herded Washington from the office. Slocum had to hope the two guards would be from Washington's company and would see that no harm came to their sergeant.

"I'm needed in the field, Major!" protested Garson. "These charges are absurd. You can't relieve me of duty when you need every man to fight Dark Crow."

"It is unfortunate, Lieutenant. Further, you are restricted to the post and you will not carry a weapon. You will have no contact with Private Washington."

"But—" Garson sputtered, then shot a venomous look at Slocum.

"Dismissed."

Garson did a smart about-face and left his commander's office.

"I find myself on the horns of a dilemma, Slocum," the major said. "The Apaches are causing seven kinds of hell all around Fort Selden, and I need both those men—and not in the guardhouse or suspended from performing their duty."

"Garson murdered my partner. He'll try to kill Washington because he's a witness."

"And what of yourself, Slocum?"

"I can take care of myself." Slocum looked like a coiled spring ready to unwind.

"I'm not sure I want you and Garson within a mile of each other." Cavendish sighed, reached into his top drawer and took out a small tin box. He drew out a sheaf of greenbacks and counted through them quickly before pushing them across his desk.

"What's that?"

"The reward I offered for the return of Benjamin Washington. Fifty dollars."

"I'm not a bounty hunter," Slocum said. "I need him to testify against Garson."

"You've got a one-track mind, Slocum. Take the money and get off the post. I'll sort all this out. I promise you justice will be served."

Slocum took the money and stuffed it into his shirt pocket. He heard the ring of determination—and truth—in Cavendish's words. But he wouldn't give the major unlimited time to work out the facts. It was as bad keeping Washington in the guardhouse as it was letting Garson walk free.

"Justice had better be quick," Slocum warned.

"Justice will be served," Cavendish said coldly. "You are dismissed, also, Mr. Slocum." The major turned back to his paperwork as Slocum left, wondering how far the officer's control over his junior officers extended.

8

Slocum left Fort Selden and rode directly to Mineral Springs. The night swept around him and turned the desert into a shadowy alien place filled with sights and sounds that were completely hidden in the hot sun.

Slocum found himself jumping at sounds he normally would have ignored, but the promise of Dark Crow and his Apaches on the warpath had put the entire countryside on edge.

Slocum was no exception.

He rode down the main street of Mineral Springs and turned to the town square, trying to get his bearings. He had left Caroline with Maybelle but doubted the woman had stayed long, since her mother was already in town. Giving up on trying to figure where Caroline might be, he set his sights on the boardinghouse at the edge of town where Maybelle Washington stayed. If Caroline was not here, Maybelle would know where she could be found.

More than this, Slocum had business to tend to with Mrs. Washington.

He dismounted in front of Miz Perkins's boardinghouse but had hardly gone halfway up the walk when the door opened.

"Good evening," Slocum said politely to the high-strung proprietress.

"You came back," Miz Perkins accused. "She's not here. She's gone, long gone!"

"Mrs. Washington?"

"You want to see *her* and not that other hussy?"

"Watch your tongue," Slocum snapped. He was in no mood for the woman to go badmouthing Caroline Thornton. He had almost died in the desert finding Benjamin Washington and had not been happy with the outcome at Fort Selden. Listening to such abuse from the disagreeable woman did not set well with him.

Miz Perkins sniffed, gathered her skirts and vanished back into her house. Slocum noticed she did not close the door so he went up and poked his head inside, almost expecting her to whack him with a broom. Maybelle worked peeling potatoes at a low table to one side of the kitchen.

"Can I have a word with you, Mrs. Washington?" Slocum called. The woman looked up, licked her lips as if this was a hard decision, then wiped her hands on her apron and hurried over to the door.

"We have to be quick about it. Miz Perkins is mighty upset over something and is like to take it out on me."

"I wanted you to know I tracked down your husband," Slocum said. He laughed wryly. "The truth is, he found me and saved my life."

"That's my Benjamin," Maybelle said, a tiny smile curling the corners of her lips.

"He's back at Fort Selden right now and wanted you to have this." Slocum fished in his pocket and drew out the wad of greenbacks Major Cavendish had given him as reward.

"Why, whatever is this for?"

"He got it when he returned to the post," Slocum said obliquely. Seeing she was not understanding, he went on.

"If he hadn't returned, he wouldn't have gotten this."

"It's back pay?"

"He wants you to have it," Slocum said resolutely.

"Well, I do declare. This will help. It's more than I get in a year from her." Maybelle tipped her head toward the rear of the house. "Course she gives me room and board, too, but this is a fortune. Thank you, Mr. Slocum." Maybelle tucked it away in an apron pocket. "I feel almost as rich as that officer."

"What?" Slocum wasn't sure he had heard the woman right. "Which officer's that?"

"Why, Benjamin's company commander. That awful Lieutenant Garson. He's all the time flashin' money round like it was nuthin' much. You'd think the Army paid him like a prince."

Slocum wondered about this but had to ask another question. "Do you know where Caroline—Miss Thornton—is?"

Maybelle smiled and looked at him. "She's sweet on you, Mr. Slocum. Or shouldn't I say that? But then you're the one askin' after her, aren't you?"

"Is she in Mineral Springs?"

"She and her ma went on back to the ranch. Mr. Thornton and his foreman came by for them not an hour ago. You might catch up with them if you hurry. They'd take yonder road back to their spread." Maybelle pointed toward the only road leading eastward, as if Slocum couldn't find it himself.

He might have gone after Caroline and her parents if Maybelle had not mentioned how Garson seemed to be rolling in cash. That worried him, and he was not sure why. It had to mean trouble brewing that he had no idea about.

"Thanks," Slocum said. "I'll pay my respects to Miss Thornton later. I need to return to the post right now."

"But it's almost dark," Maybelle said. "I'm sure Miss

Caroline would be glad to see you, no matter what time of day—or night—it was."

In spite of Maybelle Washington playing matchmaker, Slocum began to get antsy about returning to Fort Selden and seeing if the woman's husband was secure in his cell.

"I'll call on her as soon as I can," Slocum promised. He hurried to the swaybacked horse he had appropriated after Washington had been put in the guardhouse. It was a cavalry mount, but no one had noticed as he had ridden from the fort.

The horse knew the way back to Fort Selden on its own, letting Slocum stew in his own juices. After what seemed to take hours, Slocum got back to the sentries at the main gate leading into the fort.

"Mr. Slocum, you back already?" called one guard. Slocum did not recognize him as having been on duty earlier but he must have been to know Slocum was returning.

"I need to talk to Washington right away."

"Well, you shore won't have no trouble findin' him. That there's the guardhouse," the sentry said, pointing to the low building set at the corner of the post. "You can't jist barge on in without the officer of the day okayin' you, though."

"Who's that?" Slocum said, a sinking feeling in the belly. His stomach turned over when he heard the answer.

"Why, Lieutenant Porter's got the duty."

"Come with me," Slocum snapped in his best command voice. He did not wait to see if the sentry obeyed or if he sounded a warning to the others in the fort. Slocum galloped for the guardhouse and hit the ground before the horse had come to a halt. He staggered a few paces and hit the guardhouse wall hard.

Spinning around, Slocum got to the door and froze. The door stood ajar. On the floor he saw a booted foot. He drew his six-shooter, then kicked the door open all the way. By now the sentry and four others had caught up with him.

"You got to have permission to get in there," the guard said. Then he saw the body on the prison floor.

"Back me up," Slocum said, slipping around the door and into the main room of the guardhouse. His stomach knotted now when he saw that both guards had been killed, their throats cut and their scalps taken. Slocum's eyes rose slowly as he took in the prisoner in the first cell.

Benjamin Washington looked big even in death. His knuckles were skinned and had bled before he died, showing he had put up a fight. Two knife wounds in his barrel of a chest had ended his life before he had been scalped.

"Injuns!" cried the sentry. "Spread the alarm. Dark Crow's comin' after us and has done kilt three of us!"

The other guards ran off shouting the warning. In a few seconds the entire troop was pouring out of barracks, half-dressed and carrying rifles.

Slocum stepped over one corpse on the floor and went to Washington. From the spatters of blood on the cell walls, it was clear he had put up quite a fight before being knifed.

"He must have worked over his attacker something fierce," Slocum said.

"He was a good man," the guard behind Slocum said. " 'Bout the best damned sergeant on the post."

"What's going on here?" came the loud demand. Standing in the doorway, saber drawn, Lieutenant Porter looked around the guardhouse. "My God, they're dead!"

"Where's Garson?" demanded Slocum.

"In his quarters. The major suspended him," said Porter. "But then you know it. You're the one who made those false accusations against him."

Slocum pushed Porter out of the way and stormed to the officers barracks. He kicked in the door, ready to shoot if Garson showed the slightest sign of fight. To Slocum's disgust, Garson lay on his bunk, a book in his hands.

"Don't you ever knock, Slocum? It's rude to burst in like that. Even a hick like you should know that."

Slocum knocked the book from Garson's hands. The man was out of uniform. Slocum's finger stabbed down and pressed into a spot on Garson's long johns.

"Blood," he said. "Fresh blood. From one of the guards or is that from Washington when you knifed him?"

"There you go making wild accusations again," Garson said. "I don't know what you're talking about."

"Where's your uniform?"

"Being cleaned. It was dirty and since I'm not on active duty, thanks to you, I—"

"Trying to get the blood out it? Washington put up quite a fight." Slocum grabbed the man's wrist and lifted, exposing cuts and bruises on the underside of Garson's right arm.

"I got that in the line of duty. And if anything's happened to Washington, you ought to be glad. The nigger killed your partner. You ought to give whoever did it a medal, though I suspect it was Dark Crow and his braves."

"Why?" Slocum demanded.

"Because they were scalped," called Lieutenant Porter from the door.

"He couldn't have known that if he didn't have anything to do with the killings," said Slocum.

"He didn't say he knew it, just that a soldier's most likely killer'd be an Apache," Porter said.

"Who else on the post has been killed? Only the three in the guardhouse?" asked Slocum.

"I wish that were so," Porter said. "We found the post doctor dead, too. Just like the other two and our prisoner. Stabbed and scalped. There's going to be hell to pay for this. The Apaches shouldn't be able to sneak in and kill us in our sleep."

"See that the guards are disciplined severely," Garson

said from his bunk. He stared at Slocum and smirked.

"Where do you get all your money?" Slocum asked. The question took Garson by surprise.

"What do you mean?"

"You're always flashing a wad of money big enough to choke a cow. Do they pay a cavalry lieutenant that well?"

"I—" Garson sputtered for a moment, then recovered his wits. "You must be referring to the monthly allowance from my family. They are quite rich and send me a stipend while I'm doing my duty defending our country at this dreary frontier post."

Slocum knew a lie when he heard it, but there was no way of calling Garson on it. He pushed past Porter to step into the cold night air. It felt as if he could not breathe in the officers barracks. Outside was hardly better.

All around ran soldiers shouting orders and hunting for Apaches that didn't exist. Slocum went to Major Cavendish's quarters adjoining the barracks, although without proof against Garson, he did not expect the officer to do anything.

And he didn't.

9

"I'm sorry, John," Caroline said, holding his arm and leaning her head against his shoulder. "Papa is usually more accommodating, especially when I ask nice."

"I can't fault him for not wanting to take on more hands right now," Slocum said. He had asked Caroline's father for a job riding herd and had been turned down flat. If the man had thought there was anything between Slocum and his daughter, he didn't let on. Slocum doubted he had an inkling about how Caroline felt, even if she had tried to sweet talk him into giving Slocum a job.

"There're so few now, he really does need extra hands. Especially ones not afraid of the Apaches," Caroline said positively.

"From the sound of it, he doesn't have much of a herd left." It was like that with most all the ranchers. The Apaches had preyed on their beeves until only the scrawniest—or the fastest—remained to roam the range. It might be a good year for fodder but it was terrible when it came to surviving the Indians. And that went double for cowboys riding the open range.

"I know he is worrying about paying the bills," Caroline admitted. "You could help so much. I know it. I ought to—"

"Don't," Slocum said. "Your pa knows his business. This year might be tough, but he can get through it."

"Only if Dark Crow is chased back to the reservation," Caroline said.

Slocum said nothing to that. He doubted Dark Crow would ever be caught, much less forced back onto the San Carlos over in Arizona. He and Victorio shared that disdain for enforced settlement on land not fit for a gila monster.

With men like Benjamin Washington being killed at Fort Selden, Slocum doubted the cavalry post would be very effective in holding down the Apache uprising. His bile rose as he thought of Washington and how he and the other soldiers had died. He was the only one questioning how Apache raiders could sneak in, kill men in the guardhouse and the lone doctor, then leave without so much as being seen. Their choice of victims was odd, and not stealing rifles or other supplies even odder.

Garson had wanted Washington out of the way and had killed him. Why had he also killed the post doctor? Had the man seen the slaughter? Slocum grew distant as he thought on why Garson had wanted to kill him. He was sure the lieutenant had tried to shoot him in the back, and Degraff had been unlucky enough to catch the bullet. Perhaps Garson had intended to backshoot both of them. Washington just had been in the wrong place and had to be killed, too, when Slocum returned him to the post.

A lot of unlucky men—and the cause of their foul luck went back to Garson.

"John? John!"

"What? Sorry, I was just thinking of other places to find a job."

"Then you're not going to ride on?" The look on the brunette's face was like the sun coming out from behind clouds on a dark and dismal day. Suddenly, all was cheerful.

"There has to be a job going begging in Mineral Springs. After all, the townsfolk are pulling out and moving elsewhere to avoid the Apaches."

"You might try Mr. Trevor at the stagecoach depot."

"There's a stage that comes to Mineral Springs?" Slocum realized there had to be. Fort Selden was only one of a string of forts built along stagecoach lines to protect the mail and insure steady supply from larger towns, although it was hardly more than a day's ride from Mesilla to the south.

"Supply trains, too," Caroline said. "You might get a job guarding one of them, though that would be terribly dangerous. The Apaches try to steal all the food rather than grow it themselves."

Slocum didn't bother telling her the Apaches were renegades and away from the reservation where they might plant crops. If they didn't steal it, they had to hunt for it and that slowed down a fast-moving band of raiders. Even Garson could find them if they pitched camp long enough to do a proper hunt and dress out their kill.

"Reckon I'll go into Mineral Springs and see what your Mr. Trevor has to say," Slocum said.

"Right now?" Caroline asked impishly. She looked toward the barn, then back at Slocum.

Caroline had her mind on one thing but Slocum knew it wasn't going to happen, even if he was willing, too. Her father sat on the front porch watching like a hawk.

"I'll get the job, then let you know the details," Slocum said. "Might be Trevor has all the shotgun messengers and drivers he can use. I'll have to find something else, then."

"Oh, he is always hunting for good men," Caroline said. In a lower voice she added, "Poor Mr. Trevor. He's hunting for a good man, and I've already found one." She gave his arm a squeeze and started to kiss him but Slocum turned slightly so she could see how her father stared at them.

"Goodbye, Mr. Slocum," she said loudly. "I hope you have better luck finding a job in town."

Slocum started to speak, then found his voice gone for a brief second when Caroline reached down and grabbed his crotch to give it a squeeze.

"Something to think about and bring you back," she whispered.

"Ma'am." Slocum tipped his hat and mounted the swaybacked nag he had kept after Washington had been locked up at the fort. The old horse moved slow but kept a steady pace, no matter what. After being on horses unable to stand the desert heat. Slocum appreciated such a reliable mount.

He reached Mineral Springs a little before sundown. The town was closing for the night, but Slocum found Horace Trevor in the stage office at the south side of the town plaza. He tethered his sturdy horse at the side and went in. The stagecoach agent jumped as Slocum entered, hand flashing for a battered Smith & Wesson on the counter.

"Sorry, mister. You spooked me."

"It didn't take much," Slocum said. "Are you always this jumpy?"

"Today has been a terrible day. There was another one. Another, can you believe it?" The short, balding man pushed wire-rimmed glasses up on his sweaty nose and flapped his arms like a bird trying vainly to fly.

"What's that?"

"Sorry, sorry, I keep forgetting not everyone knows. Nobody in town, actually. I shouldn't tell you, either."

"I'm looking for a job," Slocum said. "It sounds as if you need someone handy with a six-gun."

"What's that? Yes, that's it. I'm sorry, this is so upsetting, so awful."

"A robbery?"

Horace Trevor took a deep breath and settled his nerves with a deep pull on a bottle from the bottom drawer of his desk. He looked longingly at the almost empty bottle, then put it back, closed then drawer and then faced Slocum.

"Yes. This afternoon, not an hour or two ago. A man riding through to Albuquerque saw the wrecked stage a few miles outside town."

"Did you tell Major Cavendish? He could have a company of men out on the robbers' trail by now."

"I tried to interest the soldiers, but that lieutenant told me there was nothing to be done."

"Garson?"

"Why, yes, Lieutenant Garson. How did you know?" Trevor cocked his head to one side, adjusted his glasses again and then said, "You're the gent who caught the deserter."

"I'm Slocum."

"You might be the man I need to ride guard on my shipments. I'm not getting any satisfaction from the cavalry. Can you find what happened to my stage?"

"A few miles down the road? That's all?" asked Slocum.

Trevor bobbed his head as if it had been mounted on a spring, then mopped his forehead. It was hot in the office but not that hot. Slocum realized how much pressure the station manager must be under.

"Are you losing a lot of stages?"

"Not so many, but the ones that matter. Those all seem to be robbed. How do they do it?"

"They? The Apaches?"

"Who else, who else? They shoot up supply trains and my stages. Why can't they get Dark Crow back where he belongs, on the reservation?"

Slocum spent a few more minutes dickering with Trevor on a salary, then left the depot and turned his pony's face southward. The sun was finally setting and the cool wind whipping along the road wiped away the last traces of sweat from Slocum's face.

It took an hour of riding before he saw the stagecoach tipped on its side alongside the narrow road. He made sure his six-shooter rested easy in his holster—although the real danger had long passed—then he rode over. Slocum dismounted and went to see if anyone had survived.

"Hello!" he called. "Anyone left alive?" He didn't want the driver or shotgun guard opening fire on him if he scared them. "Horace Trevor sent me."

As he neared the coach, he saw one passenger still inside. From the crazy angle of his head to the rest of his body, Slocum knew he was long dead. Crawling up the side of the coach, Slocum went forward to the driver's box. Curled up in the bottom, wedged in and unmoving, was the guard. Slocum hunted for the strongbox but didn't find it. He dropped to the ground and looked over the stagecoach. The luggage in the boot had been jerked out and the contents rifled through. Nothing of the clothing scattered around must have appealed to the Apache raiders.

As that thought crossed his mind, Slocum began a more thorough study of the ground around the stage. He found hoofprints, but the sun and wind had obscured them so much he could not tell whether they were coming or going or anything about the horses or the riders. The real discovery was two sets of footprints leading into the desert.

A hundred yards away he found the driver. The man had been shot in the back and had stumbled this far before dying. Slocum patted his pockets, hunting for anything that might be of worth to the next of kin. The driver's pockets were empty save for a small pouch of tobacco and a few rolling papers.

"All down but one," Slocum said, seeing that a set of

prints continued from here. A passenger must have escaped with the driver from the carnage back at the road. The faint starlight made tracking difficult but Slocum kept at it, intent on finding a survivor who could tell him what had happened. Details did not fit, and Slocum was at a loss to explain why he had the feeling this was more than it appeared.

For more than two hours he followed the tracks, occasionally losing them and finding them again more by luck than skill. As he topped a sandy rise, Slocum's sixth sense warned him to be more cautious. Rather than walk the ridge, he stayed low and surveyed the rocky, sandy stretch beyond.

A man struggled not a hundred yards away, pulling himself along since his leg appeared to be injured. Slocum guessed this was the lone surviving passenger but held back from shouting out to him. He was glad he was so wary.

A loud whoop cut through the still desert night as another indistinct figure came riding up. Slocum drew his six-shooter, but the range was too great to get a good shot at the Apache. The Indian bent low and swung his rifle barrel against the other man's head. Even from this distance Slocum heard the sick crunch of metal breaking bone.

The stagecoach passenger tumbled facedown onto the desert floor. The Apache wheeled his horse about and came back. He jumped to the ground and poked his victim with the muzzle of his rifle. When he got no response, the brave let out another whoop and danced around, then dropped, one knee in the middle of the prone man's back. The silver flash of a knife as it caught starlight alerted Slocum to what was happening.

Again he lifted his six-shooter, but the distance was too great. And again caution saved him. Three more Apaches rode up as the first brave finished scalping the downed man. They circled the dead man a couple times, then the four warriors rode off into the night.

Slocum lay on the ridge for almost twenty minutes, waiting to see if they would return. He doubted they were laying a trap, but they might fetch others to view the kill, such as it was. When it became apparent the Indians were long gone, Slocum made his way to the dead man's side.

He had seen enough scalped men in his day not to mind that much, but the other wounds were what revolted him. The man had been shot in the back no fewer than three times.

By the Apache? Slocum had not heard any shots as he approached the struggling passenger. The Apaches might have used him for their own cruel amusement, but Slocum was sure he would have heard gunfire as he crossed the still desert.

As he had done with the driver, he patted the man's pockets looking for something to identify him. His pockets were empty, too, as if he had been robbed. Slocum frowned, reconstructing all he had seen from the ridge. The Apache had knocked the man to the ground with his rifle. While he might have found valuables, the brave hadn't appeared to search the fallen man.

The Indian had taken his life and his scalp and that was all.

With the Apaches roaming the area, Slocum wasn't inclined to drag the man's body back to the stagecoach so someone could fetch it back to Mineral Springs for a proper burial. Slocum got his bearings the best he could, backtracked, again got his bearings next to the dead driver and finally returned to the stage.

A final inspection showed that the strongbox and anything of value was gone.

All the way back to Mineral Springs Slocum chewed on everything he had found. Somehow, he wasn't surprised to see that Horace Trevor was still in his office.

Slocum brushed off dust as he went in. Trevor jerked erect, his hand reaching for the pistol on the counter.

"Mr. Slocum!" the agent said with relief. "What did you find? You're back so quick."

"You were right that the stagecoach was only a few miles outside town. You have a map?"

"Right here." Trevor spread a tattered, faded Army map on the counter so Slocum could mark the location of the stage, the driver and the dead passenger.

"I found the last man here," Slocum said. "An Apache scalped him while I watched. There wasn't anything I could do since the brave wasn't alone. I counted more four braves and think there might have been others nearby."

"Oh, my. More Apaches," groaned Trevor. "How will I ever get my shipments through?"

"What was in this one?"

"The strongbox held a shipment of cash for the bank. Perhaps a thousand dollars. I thought it would be safe with the driver and a guard. Oh, those awful Indians!"

Slocum frowned as he chewed over what he had seen— and not seen.

"There wasn't much evidence that Apaches attacked the stage," Slocum said.

"But you saw a passenger killed by one of those awful redskins!"

"Some distance away from the road," Slocum allowed. "There weren't any arrows in the stage, and the strongbox was gone. Indians might have opened it right there. Why take it when it would slow them down?" Slocum did not add that he found it suspicious that an Apache would steal gold. They had nothing but disdain for the metal and had never understood the white man's lust for it.

"Dark Crow might have all the rifles and ammo he can use. Why shoot arrows when you can gun down a man from a safe distance? No, Mr. Slocum, the Indians did this. They massacred all those poor people." Trevor moaned and put his face in his hands. He was taking it hard.

Slocum said nothing about how Apaches were always careful with their ammo because all of it had to be stolen. The brave out on the desert had not shot the passenger, preferring to knock him to the ground and finish him with a knife. But if Apaches had robbed the stage, they had seen fit to shoot the man at least three times in the back. Why let him and the driver escape?

Not much of it made sense. Then Slocum decided nothing about Apache raiders followed a remotely logical path. They were too intent on killing any white man and staying off the reservation to make sense in what they did.

Still, everything about the robbery bothered Slocum.

10

"It must be the Apaches. That's what Mr. Trevor said, isn't it?" asked Caroline Thornton. She settled her skirts around her as she sat on the rock high above the Thornton spread. They had ridden into the mountains and had found this out-of-the-way spot to look at the sunset. Caroline might have been staring at the bright oranges and reds dancing along the clouds to the west but Slocum found himself more interested in her.

She was about the only thing he had found around Fort Selden that he understood.

"Trevor said it was Apaches, but I think it was road agents."

"But you saw the brave kill that poor man!"

"He had been shot in the back three times. The Apache could have shot him again but chose to save his ammo. More than that, how did the passenger escape so far into the desert if the Apaches were after him? He and the driver were on foot. The Apaches were mounted."

"I can't see them letting anyone go, unless they wanted some brutal sport," Caroline said. The brunette pushed back her hair from her face. The tumble of rippling hair turned chestnut colored in the rays of the dying sun. The soft, warm light ran along her profile and made Slocum even more intent on her, rather than the scenery stretched before them.

She was a gorgeous woman, and he had not ridden back to the Thornton ranch to discuss the stagecoach robbery. There had been no time before for what he thought she wanted—and what he wanted, too.

"I've been working with Maybelle and other Negro women who have menfolks at the fort," Caroline said. "They all complain how difficult it is."

"Bad food, terrible officers," Slocum said, his mind only half on what Caroline was saying. The light caressed her crisp white blouse and accentuated the thrust of her breasts. A button had come loose at her throat, showing the barest hint of snow white flesh. She idly reached up and played with the next button. It fell open. As she half turned toward him, the next button came undone, also, revealing the creamy swell of bare breasts.

"What is it, John? You're looking at me so strangely."

"Like a wolf who's found his prey," Slocum said, scooting closer to her. Caroline started to say something more. Slocum wasn't having any of it. He knew what he wanted and intended to deliver what Caroline wanted, as well.

He kissed her.

She recoiled in surprise, then broke the kiss. A sly smile danced on her lips.

"I wondered if you would get the idea."

"You give me all kinds of ideas," he said, kissing her again. Caroline sighed and threw back her head when his mouth left hers and slowly traveled down the line of her jaw to her delicate throat. He found the hollow between her collarbones and kissed there before moving lower. He had to unbutton more of her blouse before her breasts tumbled out freely in the cool twilight.

He made sure they had no time to get cold. Slocum's

lips curled around the cherry red nub atop her left breast and gave it a good tongue lashing. Every time his tongue laved her nipple, he felt a new ripple of desire course through her trim young body. Before she had a chance to complain how he was spending too much time on just one breast, Slocum slid wetly down into the deep canyon between those succulent mounds and slowly spiraled up the left breast. He didn't want to miss a single square inch of such soft, wondrous flesh.

"Oh, yes, John. I'm on fire inside. I'm burning up like the noonday desert sand!"

He caught at the other nub and sucked it into his mouth. His teeth raked along the sensitive button and caused Caroline to thrust her chest out boldly, trying to stuff it all into his mouth. It was a losing proposition, but they both enjoyed the way he tried and the way she moved about in front of him.

Slocum backed off and dropped to his knees so he could lift her skirts. The brunette parted her knees widely, wantonly, in silent invitation of what was to come. Slocum ran his hands under the mountains of cloth and pushed it all away to expose her privates. The soft curled nest beckoned to him.

He dived down, and as he had all over Caroline's breasts, he applied his tongue to the tender nether lips he found there.

If the tremors in her body had been obvious before, now they were earthquakes. Every time he lapped and licked at her, the brunette shivered in pure delight. She draped one leg over his shoulder so he was able to move in even closer. Caroline rocked back and supported herself on her elbows as he avidly applied his mouth and tongue to everything he found nestled between her soft white thighs.

"I . . . I can't take much more, John. I'm burning up inside. You've turned me into a wild woman!"

He kissed her thighs as he moved up her body again. The layers of skirt got in his way, and Caroline was shaking too much from desire to push them out of the way.

"Do it now, John. Take me now. I need you so!"

Slocum dropped his gun belt and began working at his jeans to free himself. Caroline said she needed him. He had to have her. It was painfully tight in his pants, and he had to get free or explode. When the last button on his fly popped free, he snapped to attention like any soldier in the army.

He looked down at the eager woman and wondered what to do. For all his need, he had not planned well. They should have brought blankets or something to soften the hard, rocky ground.

Caroline saw the problem immediately. Her sly smile turned into a broad grin as she rolled over and pushed to her feet, leaning forward. The round white curves of her shapely ass waggled enticingly in the air.

"Go on, hurry," she cried. "I can't stand not having you inside me!"

Slocum stepped up, grabbed the woman's hips and pulled her back into his groin. His heavy loglike organ parted her fleshy cheeks and then moved lower until he felt the heat and dampness welling from her inner core. Caroline reached back between her legs and took him in hand.

It was Slocum's turn to gasp. She squeezed down on his hardness a few times, then tugged gently to position him. He felt her pinkly scalloped hidden lips part around the tip of his manhood, then he pistoned forward with a thrust that carried him full-length into her seething interior.

This time they both cried out in joy. Slocum felt crushed by her tightness, and Caroline was filled with his steely shaft. He reached down and gripped her hips a little tighter, squared his feet for support, then began thrusting quickly and retreating slowly from the paradise he found.

Every time Slocum moved forward, he sank into a heated velvet glove that caressed his length. He hardly wanted to leave, but he did so that he could rush back in. The way Caroline moaned and sobbed in pleasure and then began thrusting her hips to meet his inward plunge began to take its toll on him.

When she started rotating her hips in a clockwise direction, he went the other direction. Every movement, no matter how slight, stimulated both of them to the breaking point.

"Hurry, John, hurry. More, more," she gasped out.

Slocum bent over and reached around her so he could fondle a dangling breast. He caught a lust-hard nipple between thumb and forefinger and tweaked hard every time he shoved himself into her hungrily awaiting center. The combination of stimulations set off Caroline like a stick of exploding dynamite.

She gasped, then slammed her hips back so hard Slocum thought he was going to cleave her in two. Nothing of the sort happened. He felt a long, steady shudder pass through her body. He kept up the rhythms of his lovemaking, tweaking her nips, slipping fast and hot between her nether lips all the way to her core. Panting, she settled down for a moment, then gave as good as she got.

Slocum thought a hand was crushing down on him every time he thrust forward. The sleek curves of her bottom melted into the sweep of his groin, forming a perfect fit. Caroline reached back down between her legs and stroked over his dangling balls whenever he got close enough. She did this only a few times because Slocum was moving fast now, the carnal friction burning at both of them.

"Yes, oh, again, yes, yes!" Caroline cried. She erupted in ecstasy once more. This time she took Slocum with her. Locked together they rocked back and forth until Slocum was no longer able to continue. He sank down and let Caroline drop flat onto the rock that had supported her.

"That was incredible," she said. The brunette rolled over on the rock and lounged back like a lizard sunning itself, but the sun had already vanished beyond the distant mountains. "I'm still on fire inside."

"And I'm about tuckered out," Slocum said.

Caroline pulled her skirts up again and let her knees drift apart to give him a good look, then coyly lowered her dress.

"If that's the way you want to be," she said primly.

"No, it's not. Why not coax me a mite?" Slocum moved forward, his limp organ swinging in the cool night air. Caroline reached out and guided him forward so she could take him into her mouth. Before long they repeated their earlier lusty lovemaking.

"It's a good thing you found work, Mr. Slocum," Caroline's father said. "There's not much call for cowboys anymore." The dejection in the man's voice told Slocum of all the trouble and pain that all the ranchers had gone through.

"Are you getting much help from the fort?" Slocum asked as he shoveled in another mouthful of steak. Thornton was killing off his herd rather than letting the Apaches steal what remained of the beeves. It was about the best meat Slocum had tasted in years. Or was it the company making it seem all the tastier? He felt Caroline's foot moving up and down his leg from where she sat across the table from him. She was a perfect picture of propriety, but they had put that notion to rest with all they had done that evening up on the hillside.

"Not much. Major Cavendish is a fine officer, but he is always being called away to be told how to do his job by his superiors. He leaves that fool Garson in command," Thornton said.

"The soldiers despise the man," Caroline said, fire in her eyes. Slocum noticed that her foot stopped moving on his leg as she built up a head of steam. "The families of the soldiers are even worse off. Garson does nothing to help them!"

"I wish you'd mind your own knitting, Caroline," Thornton said. "Don't go mingling with those Negroes. No good will come of it."

"Father, please," Caroline said testily. "They would get along just fine without anyone's help if Garson didn't cut off their husbands' pay."

"That's a problem on all cavalry posts," Slocum said. "Payrolls are hard to meet when the Army doesn't send the money."

"I think they get it, but Garson steals it," Caroline said positively.

"She don't know nuthin' for sure," Thornton said, looking at his daughter in an attempt to quiet her. "What we do know for sure is that Garson is always north when the Apaches are raiding south. When he heads south, you can bet your bottom dollar Dark Crow's on his way north."

"It wasn't like that when Sergeant Washington was in the field," Caroline said.

Thornton heaved a deep sigh and nodded agreement. "He was one fine soldier, that I'll grant. Pity about his wife being made a widow at such a young age, but this is frontier."

"It might be a little more civilized if the cavalry did its job," Slocum said. His mind raced. "Horace Trevor says getting shipments from the bank in Mesilla is devilishly hard because of the holdups."

"Apaches," Thornton said.

Slocum started to contradict him but held his tongue. Dark Crow and his braves had committed enough atrocities to last a lifetime, but the robbery and murders of those on the last stagecoach weren't the doing of the

Apaches. Slocum would bet on that, although he had no proof. Too many details were wrong for it to be easily blamed on the rampaging Indians.

"Mr. Slocum, will you help me with aid for the soldiers' families?" asked Caroline.

"Caroline, please, don't get Mr. Slocum mixed up in your cockamamie schemes."

"No, sir, she's right," Slocum said. "There's one thing I can do that will help everyone around Fort Selden."

"What do you have in mind?" asked Thornton.

"Seeing that Garson gets what he deserves is a start," Slocum said, polishing off the last of his steak.

11

Slocum was not happy with the notion that the stagecoach robbery had been committed by Apaches. He could not deny that an Apache brave had killed the surviving passenger, but nothing else about the robbery made sense. He turned his swaybacked horse—he thought of it as his own now, a legacy of Benjamin Washington—toward the main gate leading into Fort Selden. The guard stepped out into the hot sunlight from a shady spot and waved at him.

"Howdy, Mr. Slocum. You comin' on back to scout fer us? We're in sore need of yer services."

The private scratched himself as he squinted up at Slocum.

"I need to talk to the major. Is he in?"

"Officers don't go tellin' me much. Officer of the day's Lieutenant Porter. You want me to fetch him?"

Slocum sucked in his breath and held it. He wasn't sure Porter was the man to talk to about stagecoach robberies. Garson and the other lieutenant looked to be in cahoots, and they might be the real power at Fort Selden.

"Mind if I just ride on over to the major's office and check for myself? You can watch me to make certain I don't steal any of your cannon."

The private laughed and waved Slocum on into the fort. The parade gound was even dustier than Slocum remembered. And bloodier. Muddy spots had been formed as blood fell from whatever victim Garson had placed in the stocks to one side of the grounds.

Slocum dismounted and knocked on the major's door. He heard a grumbled "Enter" from the other side and went in.

"Slocum," Cavendish said, looking up from a mountain of paperwork. "Surprised to see you again."

"After Washington was murdered, you mean," Slocum said.

"Don't go on about that. I have disciplined Porter for his laxness in letting Apaches enter the post as they did."

Slocum knew better than to argue the point. Major Cavendish might be a good officer, but he had his weaknesses, too. A big one was not wanting to lose his junior officers. That would leave him severely shorthanded and hamper any action he might be ordered to take against Dark Crow.

That didn't excuse him letting Garson get by with murdering his own men. Two guards and the post doctor had also been killed the night Washington was assassinated.

"What have you found out about the stage robbery?" Slocum asked.

"The latest one?" Cavendish let out a sigh that turned to a shudder and then a cough that built from deep in his throat. He was paler than usual and his hands shook. Slocum wondered if the officer might not be suffering from consumption. Pressure to do his job was taking its toll on him.

The major might not have much choice keeping Garson in the chain of command if he were too ill to sortie himself.

"The stage line agent—"

"Horace Trevor," cut in Cavendish. "is an astute man.

He pinpointed the culprits right away, not that it was too hard."

"You agree with him that Dark Crow was responsible?" asked Slocum. He was disappointed with the major's too easy assessment of the robbery and the killings.

"I have to, after my men returned with evidence that the Apaches were responsible." Cavendish fumbled around in his lower desk drawer and tossed a broken arrow onto the desk. "Lieutenant Garson found that embedded in the driver's back."

Slocum looked coldly at the major, then decided there was no way the commander could know that the driver had been shot in the back—with a bullet. Slocum had checked the man's body and had not seen an arrow sticking out of him. Missing such a clue as to the attackers' identity was possible, but not this time. Slocum had been sure.

"What about the shipment?"

"The strongbox was missing," Cavendish said. "Dark Crow or his braves took it."

"For the money? For greenbacks stuffed in it?" Slocum could not hide the contempt in his voice. The Indians' contempt for the white man reached a pinnacle when it came to paper money. They did not understand the white man's drive to find gold and silver and grub it out of the rock, but those metals were useful for making jewelry and other ritual items. But paper money? Dark Crow would not even use it to light a fire, because it would never occur to him that scrip had any use at all.

"You think some group other than Dark Crow's was responsible?" Cavendish recoiled a little, not wanting to deal with any proof Slocum might have.

Rather than telling him Garson had brought in an Apache arrow and falsely claimed it had been shot into the driver, Slocum took a different path.

"You have any trouble with road agents? Whites robbing the stage? The notion of paper money would be a lot more attractive to them than to a renegade Apache on the run."

"There're always outlaws passing through the territory, but at the moment my primary mission is to catch Dark Crow and return him to the San Carlos Reservation." Cavendish spoke with such aloofness that Slocum realized the conversation was at an end unless he offered to return to scout for Cavendish.

It would be a cold day in New Mexico Territory before that happened. Slocum knew he would find himself under the orders of either Garson or Porter and would undoubtedly end up a casualty. He could even imagine the mock sorrow in Garson's voice as he dropped another Apache arrow on the major's desk and told him how Slocum had been shot in the back.

"I think you're wrong, Major" was all Slocum said as he got ready to leave.

"Wait, Mr. Slocum. You might be right that we are facing more than an Apache uprising. I remember seeing a communiqué a few months ago about an outlaw gang moving up from West Texas. I don't know what happened to the message—it had all the details—but I am not discounting the possibility we face more danger than that so generously offered up by Dark Crow."

Slocum said nothing, letting the major stew in his own juices for a spell.

"I'll send out a patrol to look into the matter more carefully. I value your opinion, sir."

"Thanks, Major." Slocum hesitated and then had to ask, "Who might be assigned this scouting foray?"

"Why, the best field commander I have. Lieutenant Garson."

Slocum thought this was the same as putting the fox to guard the henhouse but said, "That's about all I can ask, Major. Good hunting."

"And to you, Mr. Slocum. And to you." The major wiped sweat from his sallow forehead and turned a shaky hand back to signing papers before moving them from the large pile to a shorter one on the other side of his desk.

Slocum left Fort Selden straightaway but did not go far. He should report to Horace Trevor a few miles down the road at his office in Mineral Springs, but he thought his hunt might be more profitable seeing who he flushed from the fort.

A few scraggly cottonwoods hinted that a clever man might find shade and a chance to rest his horse. Slocum rode over and found a decent spot to rest and watch. For all the sad condition of the horse's back, it had a good heart and was dependable. Slocum wished that Washington was still astride the swaybacked horse and that he still had his own gelding, but he knew he might as well wish for rain and a long, cool drink from a beer barrel.

Slocum lounged back and positioned his broad-brimmed hat low on his forehead to block the sun but still give him a view of the road leading from Fort Selden. It might be a spell before Garson rode out at the head of his column. Slocum wanted to be rested when the lieutenant took to the trail, since it would be a long time before he got a chance to tarry again.

He dozed for almost an hour, until he heard a bugle call from the direction of the fort. He pushed up his hat and saw Garson with two dozen buffalo soldiers dutifully following. Slocum wondered if they had been Sergeant Washington's men. They rode with easy grace but were alert, even this close to their fort.

Slocum knew he would have big trouble on his hands if he dropped his guard for even a moment. The soldiers might not like Garson, but Washington had trained them well. They would obey their commanding officer's orders, no matter what.

Even if it meant killing a former scout like Slocum.

He mounted the swaybacked horse and set off on the trail, following at a decent distance to keep from being spotted. Before the soldiers camped for the night in the foothills of a particularly rugged stretch of mountains, Slocum saw the change in their alertness. Garson harangued them constantly, berating them for minor infractions that no one field officer would bother mentioning. The angrier his tirade, the less attentive the buffalo soldiers became. They camped and would not have put out sentries if Garson had not insisted.

"Amazing," Slocum said to himself, watching the steady deterioration of morale. Washington had left a good company, and it took Garson only an afternoon on the trail to destroy it.

The sentries knew the Apaches were not likely to attack at night and became more than careless—they were criminally guilty of sleeping at their posts. Slocum tried to imagine them doing this with Washington as their sergeant and could not.

He slipped past one dozing guard and walked halfway to the fire fitfully sputtering in the center of the camp. Slocum looked around and saw all were asleep—except Garson. The lieutenant finished cleaning his sidearm, looked around and then crept off into the night.

Slocum was quick to follow because of the way the officer moved. He wasn't going off to relieve himself. He had checked to be sure the soldiers slept.

Garson made his way up the hill to a ridge and waited for several minutes, forcing Slocum to take cover. Slocum rested his hand on his Colt, wondering if he ought to take Garson now. The officer would likely brag about how he had killed Washington, but Slocum wanted more from Garson now than an admission of guilt. He had to find out about the deaths of the passengers, driver and shotgun messenger before closing the book on Garson.

He wanted the man to stand trial and then hang for his crimes. That would give people like Maybelle Washington a chance to see that justice was done. And Slocum had never found out if the driver and guard on the stagecoach had family. They deserved to know the killer of their relatives had been brought to justice.

If he couldn't get proof that would convince Cavendish and any other officer at a court-martial, then he would take care of dispensing justice himself.

Garson paced anxiously, then set out at a trot, as if he had come to a decision. Slocum followed more slowly, carefully picking his way through the clumps of cactus and Spanish bayonet to avoid making any sound and to keep from injuring himself. Added danger lurked in moving quietly, also. The rattlesnakes the Apaches feared so would not know he was coming and might take offense if he stepped on them in the dark.

Garson vanished over the ridge. The only reason Slocum could think for the officer's strange behavior was that he was going to meet someone. If it happened to be members of the outlaw gang that had robbed the stage, Slocum could follow them to their lair and then turn every last one of the road agents over to Major Cavendish in a neatly wrapped package.

One or two of the outlaws would turn on their leader and accuse Garson to keep a hemp rope from tightening around their necks.

Slocum kept low as he reached the top of the ridge. He looked around for Garson, then cursed under his breath. The officer had disappeared, swallowed in the inky night. Ragged mountains rose in front of him, but Slocum doubted Garson had gone too far up a canyon on foot. The going would be rough and sounds from him stumbling about in the dark would echo back. All Slocum heard was the distant howl of a lovesick coyote and the gentle whistle of wind coming out of the canyon.

He squatted, waiting for Garson to reveal himself. Slocum had to wait several minutes before he heard rocks tumbling down from the left side of the canyon. He studied the dark face but saw nothing. It might be nothing more than a clumsy cougar moving or a mountain goat jumping from one ledge to another higher up on the cliff face, but Slocum doubted it. He started down the far side of the ridge and headed for the base of the sheer rock surface.

Slocum dropped to one knee when he saw a mesquite thorn with a piece of blue cloth caught to it. Garson had passed this way. Why? Slocum was certain he was meeting someone, but whoever he had intended to meet had never shown up.

Slocum's heart beat a little faster. He might be on the doorstep of the outlaws responsible for the stagecoach robbery. When they had not come to meet Garson, he had gone to them.

A wedge of darkness blacker than the surrounding rock drew Slocum. The narrow crevice led into the face of the cliff. If he went in, he would be a sitting duck. If he didn't, he would never know where Garson had gone.

Without hesitation, Slocum turned sideways and began wiggling into the rocky fissure. The cold stone sides pressed in even more, making him wonder if he had guessed wrong. Then the sides widened, and he saw a trail leading from the opening down to a small stand of trees, indicating a watering hole.

Angry voices came from the area of the trees. Slocum recognized Garson's right away.

He looked up to see if he could scale the rocks and get a better view of the small stand of trees. He saw what looked to be footholds on the rock face and quickly scaled the face like a spider on a wall. On a small ledge, he had a front-row seat as Garson and six other men gathered around a campfire argued loudly. He was a bit far off to hear clearly, but he concentrated and caught snippets of the argument.

"You were supposed to make it look like Indians did the killing. I had to find an arrow and give it to Cavendish. It's damned lucky he's so stupid that he believed me," Garson said.

"Aw, you're always pissin' 'n' moanin' 'bout something," another man said. "It wasn't our fault the driver and passenger got away. We shot 'em up. How were we to know they wouldn't die right away?"

"You should have tracked them down and scalped both of them, the way I told you," Garson said. "This is a sweet deal we have, as long as Dark Crow is raiding. I don't want you messing it up because you're getting careless."

Slocum missed the answer as the men moved away and became hidden by the trees. He craned his neck and saw a higher ledge where he might get a better view. The climb would be riskier than getting to this narrow rock sill, but Slocum thought the effort was worth it. He recognized Garson's voice, but the others were strangers. If he wanted to bring them all to justice for their crimes, he had to identify them.

Strong fingers found knobs and crevices as Slocum climbed another ten feet up to a ledge that ran off into the darkness. The one below had been short. This one might provide a balcony allowing him to eavesdrop on Garson and his gang.

As he started along the ledge, rocks from above tumbled down in front of him. Slocum froze, not sure what had caused the small rock fall.

He went to the edge and looked up in time to see a lariat flicker against the background of stars in the night sky. The lasso closed about his shoulders, then tightened painfully as the man above him yanked hard.

Slocum's feet went out from under him, and he slipped off the ledge, dangling with the rope cruelly pinning his arms to his sides. He looked down at a thirty-foot drop, then jerked around so he could see the man above him.

"This is like shootin' fish in a barrel," the outlaw said, taking a couple turns of rope around a rock to secure Slocum so he could draw his six-shooter.

Slocum felt like a fish on the end of a line. He kicked frantically, to no avail. Growing more desperate, he looked up again and saw the man grinning as he sighted along the barrel of his six-gun.

The cocking six-shooter sounded like a death knell in Slocum's ears.

12

Slocum kicked hard and swung back under the rim of rock above him. For a brief instant, the danger from the gunman vanished, but Slocum saw he could not keep from swinging back out into space—and into the man's sights. Wincing, he reached behind him and grabbed the handle of his knife.

As momentum carried him back into space, Slocum slashed wildly at the rope pinning his upper shoulders. If it slipped off, it would circle his neck and hang him.

"Hey!" the guard yelled. The man tumbled backward as the weight vanished and he was left with nothing but severed rope. His shot went into the sky, but Slocum was past caring about that. He fell into the darkness of the canyon below.

Slocum gasped when he smashed into the rocky wall and bounced away. He waited for death as he slammed to the hard ground, but a spindly pine tree saved his life. Slocum crashed through its dried, dead limbs, spun around and flung out his arms to protect his face as he continued his downward plunge. He grunted when another branch cracked under his weight. And then he hit the ground with bone-crushing force.

Lying stunned, Slocum tried to get his senses back. If he didn't make tracks fast, Garson and his cohorts would come investigate the noises. The guard's shot would alert them if the sound of him falling through the tree limbs didn't.

Gasping for breath, Slocum pushed up to hands and knees. A moment's dizziness passed and let him get painfully to his feet. Slocum took a step and fell again, his leg not working right. He reached down and touched his thigh. His fingers came away wet with blood.

"Over there," came the distant command. "See where the son of a bitch went!"

Slocum pulled himself back to his feet and dragged his leg behind as he retreated into the brush. He dropped to the ground and rolled and then kept rolling when he heard the guard far above on the canyon rim shouting directions for Garson to find the invader. Dizzy and disoriented, Slocum scrambled farther down the canyon in an attempt to get away. His only ally was darkness. The guard above could not see him and Garson had to track him.

Tracks. Bloody tracks. The wound on his leg bled freely. He had to stop it or Garson would follow the blood trail straight to him.

Slocum tumbled down an incline and lay panting at the bottom. Sheer determination kept him moving into a tumble of large rocks near the face of the cliff. Staying close to the wall prevented the guard above from shooting at him, although Slocum doubted the man could see anything but vague movement in the dark undergrowth. The others? Slocum would have to shoot it out with Garson and his cronies if they came upon him.

He collapsed in the tight space between two large boulders. Slocum pressed his palm into his leg but couldn't stop the bleeding. He tried to pull off his belt, but his fingers had turned too numb. Then he noticed how a piece of the rope that had been around his shoulders was still embedded in his flesh. Painfully pulling the segment out of his arm and back sent new waves of pain through him, causing him to black out momentarily.

Slocum fought his way back from the brink of unconsciousness and looped the blood-soaked length of rope around his upper thigh. It was just long enough to loop around. He cinched it down as tightly as he would the belly strap on a mustang. The bleeding stopped, but Slocum still had to fight the dizziness from loss of blood.

". . . here somewhere," came the distant words. Slocum didn't recognize the speaker. But he did the man who answered.

"He must have hightailed it. None of you yahoos is worth his salt as a tracker," Garson said.

"Get one of them black boys who follow you around like puppy dogs to go after him," said the first man. A solid thud echoed along the canyon walls. Slocum closed his eyes and imagined Garson hitting the other man for his impertinence.

The sounds faded away as Slocum slipped into a deep, dark place where nothing bothered him anymore.

Cold. He was so cold. Slocum tried to pull the blanket up around him but there wasn't one. His fingers banged against cold rock. Forcing his eyes open, he saw only browns and grays. Panicked, he sat up and immediately regretted it. He banged his head against a low rock.

But the pain focused him. He was cold and weak but still alive. Garson had not found his hidey-hole. Slocum doubted the army lieutenant had done much hunting: he'd be more willing to abandon this camp than to waste time hunting for someone who might not know or care what was going on.

Slocum was sure the men Garson had met were responsible for the stagecoach robbery. He had no proof, but in his gut he was sure.

He gripped the edge of a sharp-edged rock and pulled himself up so he could look out into the canyon. The sun shone straight down. Slocum couldn't remember when he had come after Garson, but it had been after midnight. That meant he had been unconscious for almost twelve hours. Or was it longer? Slocum couldn't think straight and had no way of knowing if he had been wedged in the rocks for a day and a half.

Knowing the danger, he crawled from his lair and to the steep slope he had fallen down. Slocum looked around, listened hard and couldn't decide if he was alone in the canyon. Squinting, he studied the canyon rim for any sign of a lookout. Nothing. He began a slow but steady climb up the gravelly slope to where he had fallen. If Garson or his gang spotted him now, he was a goner.

The longer Slocum walked, dragging his injured leg in the dirt and leaving tracks a blind man could follow, the more he thought he was alone. More by accident than design, he found the outlaws' campsite. From the look of it, they had left in a hurry. Slocum laughed harshly at the notion he had chased them off. In his condition he could not have fended off a sick kitten.

A small stream provided him with water and a chance to loosen the tourniquet on his leg. Pain lanced through him, but Slocum hung on grimly. To pass out now meant death. He cleansed the wound the best he could, then bandaged it with pieces of his pant leg and waited to see if he had to reapply the tourniquet.

In spite of the pain, the bleeding had stopped. Slocum drank some more, splashed water on his face, then limped in the direction of the crevice he had used to enter this canyon. There must have been an exit at the far end of the rock-walled retreat used by the outlaws, but that was the last place Slocum wanted to find. He had to get back to the swaybacked pony that had been Benjamin Washington's and find a doctor.

The trip that had taken him less than a half hour in the dark and moving cautiously the night before now took the remainder of the day. Slocum had to stop often, rest and then move on. He perked up around twilight when he saw the dark fissure leading out to his horse.

Slocum had barely started for the exit when he felt eyes on him. He drew his six-shooter and slowly turned to check his back trail. Eyes the color of amber peered up at him. The heavily muscled mountain lion padded forward slowly, its lips drawn back in a silent snarl.

The way it crouched, the silence of its approach, the way it looked fixedly at him told Slocum the cougar thought it had found dinner. The big cats seldom attacked men, but this one might have developed a taste for human flesh, especially since the hunting cat already scented his blood. It certainly showed no sign of fear as it advanced.

Slocum waited until he saw the powerful muscles in the hindquarters clench for a jump. Simultaneous with his first shot, he shoved himself to the side. The big cat leaped and found itself in midair, unable to change its attack. The bullet creased its front leg and elicited a loud, savage scream of pain and rage. Then the cougar fell past Slocum, missing him by inches.

Not waiting for the cat to turn and renew the attack, Slocum fired again point-blank. The bullet hit the cat in the side and brought forth an even more ferocious howl. Slocum fired again and again, but the small-caliber six-shooter was not up to the task of killing such a large animal.

The mountain lion had poised for another leap when Slocum got lucky. A bullet went into the cat's mouth and ripped through its guts. It leaped but fell far short of its intended victim.

Weak, pale and trembling, Slocum pointed his Colt Navy at the twitching cougar, then relaxed and shoved his six-gun back into its holster. The danger had passed. Slocum sank to the ground beside the big cat and marveled at his luck in killing it. One good swipe of a huge clawed paw would have ended Slocum's life in a flash.

It was darker than a coal mine by the time Slocum had regained enough strength to continue his retreat through the rock crevice. He began having nightmares of fainting here and being trapped forever. An occasional glance straight up showed a thin wedge of stars in the sky. The promise of an entire sky filled with the blazing bright points of light kept him moving.

He lurched forward and fell to hands and knees when the rocks suddenly parted and seemed to spit him out. Slocum fumbled out the watch that had been his only legacy from his brother Robert and clicked open the case.

Midnight. He had spent the last day getting shot at, dropped off a mountain, cut up by a spindly pine tree and attacked by a cougar. About all he had learned was what he already knew—that Lieutenant Garson was mixed up in more illegal activity than killing Washington, the guards and the post doctor. Slocum still had no proof of any of it, at least none that Major Cavendish would accept. It still came down to Slocum's gut feeling versus Garson's usefulness as a field commander.

"My horse," Slocum said in a voice turned to gravel. "Die if I don't find that horse." He alternately crawled and hobbled to where he had left the horse the night before. For a moment he didn't recognize the animal. Then he realized it was angry with him, pawing the ground and snorting foam.

"There, there," he soothed. "Let me on. Let me into the saddle. I know you haven't had it off in a couple days. Sorry, so sorry."

Slocum pulled himself into the saddle, got the reins wrapped around his left wrist so he wouldn't drop them, then started the swaybacked horse toward Fort Selden. It was dangerous going there, but Slocum had to have a destination in mind. It was so hard to concentrate. Major Cavendish could help, even if there wasn't a doctor there. An aide. Some of the soldiers might know how to treat him. Anything. Something.

"Home," Slocum told the horse. "Take me home."

He was never quite sure when he blacked out, but he did. Slocum slumped forward and clung to the saddle horn instinctively. The reins wrapped around his wrist did not fall and the sturdy horse plodded on, taking him to safety.

From a great distance Slocum heard a soft voice exclaim. "Glory be!" Then hands grabbed at him. He fought, not wanting to tumble from the saddle.

"You let go now, you heah?"

Strong hands pulled the reins away from him and supported him as he slid from horseback to the ground.

"Who?" he asked but his eyes refused to focus. Slocum had been drifting in and out of consciousness and only got small snippets of the world around him. Sunlight. He had ridden all night. Hands lifting him to his feet so he could stumble along.

"You lean on me now," came the voice he almost remembered. "I'll get you into the shed out back. No reason to bother Miz Perkins. What you been doin', suh? You're a perfect mess!"

"Tracked Garson," Slocum croaked. "Outlaw. He's the leader of the outlaws that robbed the stage. Tell . . ." Slocum couldn't think of who to tell. A door creaked open, and he stumbled forward and fell heavily onto a small cot.

The door might have closed. The curtains might have been drawn shut. More likely, Slocum passed out.

"How you feelin' this mornin', Mr. Slocum?"

He sat up in bed with a start. He felt lighter and knew in an instant why. His gun belt and six-shooter were hanging on a hook on the wall across the small room. And his boots. His boots were off. So were his clothes.

"Mrs. Washington," he said, blinking to clear his foggy eyes. "How'd I get here?"

"Why, that ole Pappy brought you."

"Pappy?"

"My Benjamin's horse. The one you're ridin'."

"I told the horse to take me home. It came here?"

Maybelle Washington beamed. "I reckon Pappy knows who gives him sugar cubes and carrots."

"How long have I been here?"

"Two days. It takes a powerful lot of healin' to fix all that was wrong with you." Maybelle held up Slocum's right boot and shook her head sadly. "I done what I could but this heah boot's ruined."

"How?"

"Filled with blood. Your blood from the look of the wound on your leg."

"You tended me?"

"Don't go gettin' upset now, Mr. Slocum. You ain't got nothin' I ain't seen befo'e. Course I tended you. Who else is theah to do it?"

Slocum lay back and tried to get his thoughts into order.

"I wanted to get evidence on Garson. I didn't do it, but I did see him with the rest of his gang. He supplies them information about shipments coming north from Mesilla. The cavalry's supposed to protect the stage, but I think he makes certain the troopers are patrolling somewhere else every time there's a big shipment of money to the bank."

"Seems that way," Maybelle said, sitting on a three-legged stool next to the bed. "Don't go gettin' yourself in a tizzy. You rest up now, you heah?"

"I hear," Slocum said, "but I have to—"

He started to get up, but Maybelle firmly shoved him back onto the bed.

"You behave. If you don't rest and get your strength back, I won't let you have no visitors."

"Visitors?" Slocum asked. Then he saw the broad grin on Maybelle's face. "I reckon I'd better do what you say, then," he said, his grin matching hers.

13

"I can get out of bed," Slocum complained. Then he looked past Maybelle Washington to the small door in the shed where she had kept him for the past three days and saw Caroline Thornton.

"I'd say something of yours is gettin' up, but it's not gonna be the rest of your body." Maybelle pushed him back down, patted the blanket around him and then went to the door to speak with Caroline.

Slocum did not hear what Caroline said but Maybelle responded, "I tole him if he was good, he'd get visitors. Seeing as how he's been real good, you can go on in."

The two women whispered a moment longer. Caroline laughed and came in, closing the door behind her.

"Maybelle tells me you've been healing fast. That's good." She sat on the edge of the cot, her leg pressing into Slocum's through the blanket. The attractive brunette looked down and saw the way the blanket tented up. "My, my, you are anxious to get up and about, aren't you?"

Slocum was past being embarrassed.

"She's like a prison warden."

"Maybelle can be quite determined," Caroline said. "She said you were quite badly injured. What happened? Was it Garson?"

Slocum explained all that had happened, finishing with a bitter "I didn't get one solid piece of evidence that'd stand up before a jury or at a court-martial. I reckon it's time I did something more to make sure he doesn't get away scot-free."

"John," Caroline said sharply. "You will *not* take the law into your own hands. That'd make you no better than Garson and his cronies."

"I haven't had any luck collecting evidence against him. I didn't even get a good look at the men he met out in that canyon."

"Can you return and track them?"

"It's been a week," Slocum said, shaking his head. For the first time in a week his head didn't feel as if everything in it had come loose and was rattling about. "Their tracks are long gone."

"Well, they are not," Caroline said. "Another stagecoach was robbed."

"Everyone killed?" Slocum read the answer on her somber face. "What about Dark Crow? Has Garson run him down yet?"

"The Apaches always stay just a mile too far away for the cavalry to capture them. If Benjamin had not died, he would have run Dark Crow off by now—or captured him for return to San Carlos."

"Garson has every reason to let the Apaches run free," Slocum said. "This is another reason Garson has to be stopped. How many will die because he doesn't want Dark Crow captured?"

"The stage robberies go virtually unnoticed," Caroline admitted.

"And the Apaches get blamed. Garson must have a mountain of money stashed away somewhere." As he said it, Slocum began thinking hard. Follow the money. Garson was not the sort to trust any of the outlaws in his gang with the money. The crooked cavalry officer had to know they would stuff the greenbacks in their pockets and ride for Mexico, leaving him nothing if he paid them outright.

"Garson is sitting on the stolen money," Caroline said, putting his thoughts into words. "So?"

"So I find it and wait. He has to come for it sooner or later. When he does, I get the drop on him and—"

"And nothing. He will claim he had found the money and, performing his duty, intended to return it to Mr. Trevor. You need more evidence than that."

"He has to be caught red-handed," Slocum said, seeing she was right. Garson had the winning hand unless Cavendish could be shown how his officer was double-dealing.

"The lieutenant is so annoying, too. The more I try to help the families of the buffalo soldiers, the more he blocks me. And he utterly refuses to allow me to take food or personal items to the soldiers themselves!"

"He's a cold-blooded killer," Slocum said. The buffalo soldiers had it rough. All frontier-stationed troopers did. He was more concerned with Garson's killing rampage. The renegade lieutenant thought nothing of murdering soldiers in his command, passengers and drivers of the stages, and of letting Dark Crow have his way as he rampaged across New Mexico Territory.

"How do you intend finding where he stashed all the loot?" asked Caroline.

"Follow him, as I did before. I don't think he will go out with the soldiers if he intends to tap into his treasure trove, though. Is he out on patrol now?"

"I don't know," Caroline said. She heaved a deep sigh of resignation, then a gleam came into her soft brown eyes. "Talking about him is nowhere near as much fun as seeing if you are healed—and ready for action."

Her hand slid under the blanket and found his thigh. Caroline's fingers lightly moved across the bandage until she found the hardness between his legs that had caused the blanket to tent earlier.

"Oh, you seem quite fit," she said, beginning to stroke up and down his length.

Slocum and Caroline both looked guiltily at the door as Maybelle came flying in, all flustered.

"Miss Thornton, Miss Thornton, somethin' terrible's happened!" Maybelle cried.

Caroline's hand jerked back, and Slocum sat bolt upright. Maybelle was not one to get needlessly upset.

"What's wrong?"

"Them Apaches. They're attackin' your homestead. A rider came in with the news."

Slocum pushed Caroline away and climbed from the bed. He ached all over, but this was nothing compared with the hurt the Thorntons would experience if somebody didn't get help to them right away.

"Caroline, Maybelle, get over to Fort Selden. Tell the major what's going on and have him personally lead a company to your ranch. Maybelle, is it Dark Crow himself who's attacking?"

"I don't rightly know."

"Then lie to the major. Insist that you know it is Dark Crow. That's the only way he'll go himself rather than sending Garson—or Porter."

"Lieutenant Porter?" asked Caroline. "Is he in cahoots with Garson?"

"I think so." Slocum climbed into his jeans, hardly noticing how Maybelle had patched them. Slipping into his boots showed him the woman had been right about how his blood had ruined perfectly good footwear. The leather had turned stiff wherever his blood had soaked into it. There was nothing he could do about that now. He grabbed his six-shooter and strapped it on.

"Don't just stand there," he snapped. "Get out to Fort Selden and tell the major everything I said. Now!"

"John?" Caroline hung back. He kissed her quickly, then pushed her out the door. She clung to him and said, "Mother and Father are alone out there. Father sent our foreman and all the cowboys who've stayed on to round up the herd down south."

"All the more reason to hurry," he told her. He held her for a moment, then followed her outside. Swaybacked Pappy stood patiently waiting for him. Slocum saddled the horse and climbed gingerly into the saddle. His leg throbbed and his head might have passed for a rotted melon, but otherwise he was in good enough shape to ride.

Slocum made certain both Maybelle and Caroline were on their way to Fort Selden before he slid the rifle from the saddle sheath and checked it. Full magazine. Then he urged Pappy to a trot as he checked the chambers in his Colt Navy. Slocum had long since learned to reload the percussion cap pistol while on the go. The horse kept on the road leading out of Mineral Springs and to the Thornton spread while he replaced the spent rounds and then tucked away a fully loaded six-gun.

His weapons were ready for a fight. Slocum hoped he was up to it.

He turned off the main road toward the Thornton ranch and heard what he first thought was distant thunder. It took him only a couple seconds to realize it was gunfire from a full-blown battle. He was heartened by the sounds because it meant the Thorntons were still putting up spirited resistance. If Dark Crow and his renegades had killed them fast, there wouldn't be any reason to keep shooting. The Indians had shown themselves to be parsimonious when it came to their precious ammo.

Slocum galloped Pappy until the horse began to falter. He was slowing the gait and almost failed to notice two braves beside the road drawing a bead on him.

Slocum reined in hard, then threw himself forward so his head was alongside Pappy's neck. He drew his six-shooter and opened fire. Several rounds went wide, but they served their purpose. The first warrior loosed a war arrow that missed Slocum by several feet. The second brave jerked as a slug ripped through his arm, causing his rifle shot to go into the ground at his feet.

Firing until his six-shooter came up empty, Slocum rode past the two Apaches. They had been sent out as sentries to warn Dark Crow of approaching trouble. All Slocum had on his side was surprise since he could never hope to run off all the Apaches single-handedly.

Somehow, he doubted Major Cavendish would arrive from Fort Selden in time.

He went another hundred yards up the road before he saw how the Apaches had arrayed themselves around the ranch house. Slocum had expected them to remain on horseback. As he neared, he saw three braves dead in the front yard. Dark Crow had attacked and met unexpected resistance from the Thorntons. Seeing that his mounted warriors were easy targets, he had ordered them to attack on foot.

Slocum got his rifle out of the saddle sheath and levered a round into the magazine. An Apache ran along the roof of the house carrying a torch. Dark Crow intended burning out the Thorntons. Slocum lifted the rifle to his shoulder, fired, missed and fired again. His second shot, more by luck than skill, shot the torch from the Apache's hand.

Turning suddenly to see who had fired at him caused the brave to slip, fall off the roof and crash to the ground. A pair of pistols were thrust from a broken window above the fallen Apache. The six-shooters blazed and the Indian died on the spot.

The barrels vanished back into the house, reassuring Slocum that someone was still alive.

"Yee-haw!" Slocum cried, riding around and shooting at any brave foolish enough to poke up a head. He hit one and kept the rest pinned down. He had failed to count the rounds fired from the rifle but knew instinctively he was getting close to the end of the magazine.

A husky brave stood, pointed at Slocum and shouted something in Apache. The brave wore war paint and stalked toward him unafraid of the bullets whistling through the air.

Slocum knew this had to be Dark Crow. The man was convinced that no white man's bullet could touch him. Slocum intended to show him how wrong he was. His rifle came easily to his shoulder, he aimed and squeezed back on the trigger.

The hammer fell on an empty chamber. Slocum was out of ammunition.

Slocum never hesitated. He put his heels into Pappy's heaving, lathed flanks and galloped forward, launching himself into the air at just the right instant.

Slocum slammed his rifle barrel into the Apache chief's arm, knocking him aside. Then he dived from the saddle and crashed into Dark Crow. They went to the ground in a jumble, arms and legs flailing.

His wounds bothering him, Slocum was slower to get to his feet. When he did, he faced Dark Crow. The Apache held a horn-handled knife firmly, waiting for the proper instant to advance and gut his enemy.

"Die at Dark Crow's hand!" cried the chief, wanting Slocum to know who his killer was.

Slocum knew better than to match his strength with the Indian's. As Dark Crow lunged, Slocum grabbed the man's wrist and tugged, keeping the Apache chief moving forward and getting him off balance. With a quick kick, Slocum landed the toe of his boot in Dark Crow's midriff. The shock that ran all the way up his injured leg told Slocum he might as well have kicked a rock.

Not releasing the brawny wrist, Slocum kept moving and tugging. As long as he forced Dark Crow down and away, he kept the Indian off balance. This could not continue long, and both fighters knew it. The stalemate ended when Dark Crow dropped his knife and somersaulted forward, wrenching his wrist free of Slocum's grip.

The Indian came to his feet, whirled around and dived for Slocum. They went down in a heap. Dark Crow's strong hands sought Slocum's throat. Ordinarily, Slocum would have been strong enough to throw the Apache off him but not know. He gave up trying to force away the hands throttling him and instead grabbed a handful of dirt. A quick toss filled the air between them with choking, blinding dust.

Dark Crow shrieked in anger, and this caused him to inhale a goodly amount of the dust. He choked and gave Slocum the only chance he was likely to get. As the Apache chief recoiled, Slocum heaved and threw him off.

"In here, hurry!" cried Caroline's mother from the open door to the ranch house. From over her shoulder poked the twin six-shooters that had ended the other Apache's life.

Slocum took two running steps forward, then fell facedown. The six-guns blazed. Dark Crow let out a cry of pain, but looking back Slocum saw the chief was only nicked. The head wound bled like a stuck pig but was not serious.

As Dark Crow retreated under the renewed barrage from the six-guns, Slocum wiggled like a snake on his belly up the steps and pushed past the woman. Behind her stood Mr. Thornton. Slocum saw immediately why he had risked his wife's life the way he had. The man's legs were bloody from a half dozen wounds, and he could not stand without her help.

Mrs. Thornton slammed the door and let her husband poke the six-shooters out the broken windows to hold the Apaches at bay.

"Red bastards," grumbled Mr. Thornton. "When is the cavalry going to get here?"

Slocum didn't have an answer.

14

Slocum saw that Caroline's father was in extreme pain.
When his wife turned and took away her support of his
weight, the man fell, catching himself on a chair and then
sitting heavily. He looked up at Slocum with a desolate
look in his eyes.

"You're a damned fool," Thornton said.

"Arthur, don't swear," his wife said primly.

"Slocum came into hell and is going to die alongside
us. Cussing about that isn't so bad."

Slocum couldn't believe the two of them arguing over
the way the man spoke. From the hoots and hollers outside, every Apache not on the reservation was waiting to
lift their scalps. The way he had beaten Dark Crow in-
sured the chief would come after him and never stop until
either the Apache or the ranchers were dead.

From the look of the Thorntons, Slocum knew Dark
Crow was more than halfway to his goal.

"How much ammo do you have?" Slocum asked. He
drew his Colt Navy and knocked the cylinder free.

"Don't rightly know we have ammunition for that,"
Thornton said. "I've got a couple other six-shooters that
match these that you can use. Martha's right good at load-
ing."

"Get me the pistols," Slocum ordered. He looked up at the ceiling and seconds later heard the soft padding of moccasins on the roof. The Apaches intended burning them out, in spite of their first failure.

"You tell the boys in blue about our troubles?" asked Thornton. He levered himself out of the chair and leaned heavily against the wall so he could look out into the front yard. Thornton took a quick shot at an Apache warrior riding past. He missed.

"I sent Caroline and Maybelle to the fort to get Major Cavendish," Slocum said. He worried that the soldiers would be too late, even if they rode straight here. "I told her to tell the major that it was Dark Crow attacking. I figured that was about all that would pry him loose from his paperwork." Mrs. Thornton handed Slocum two .44s. He used one right away as a brave poked his head up over the windowsill to the south. Slocum blew away an eagle feather but did not wound the man.

"Not far from the truth," Thornton said. "I don't recognize him, but that one's got to be important." He took several more shots at Dark Crow as the Apache chief strutted around and yelled insults.

"It's Dark Crow," Slocum said.

"Aren't we the lucky ones," Thornton said dryly. He emptied his six-guns and passed them to his wife, who sat on the chair and dutifully reloaded.

Slocum kept his attention on the ceiling. He no longer heard the Indian on the roof but knew this line of attack would be the most advantageous. If the Apaches set fire to the roof, the entire house and everyone inside would be flushed like ducks off a pond.

"What's wrong? You got a kink in your neck?" asked Thornton.

"Your roof," Slocum said. "Any way onto it from inside?"

"Nope, no reason."

Slocum grabbed another chair and put it on the dinner table, then climbed up. He began prying loose the ceiling and discarded boards with wild abandon. A cascade of dust covered him when he broke through. Slocum took a deep breath, grabbed the edge of the small hole he had made, then heaved himself up and through.

Half-sprawled on the roof, he made an ideal target. Luck rode with him. The Apache's crude torch had gone out, and he knelt at one side of the roof, vainly trying to relight it. Slocum shoved his right hand in front of him, lifted the six-shooter and fired as the brave turned. The slug caught the Apache smack in the center of his chest. He toppled backward off the roof, taking the unlit torch with him.

Slocum wiggled on through the hole and kept low until he got to the edge of the roof. From this vantage point he fired steadily, bringing down two more warriors. He wanted a good shot at Dark Crow, but the chief was nowhere to be seen.

"Mr. Slocum!" called Mrs. Thornton. "Do you need a reload?"

He looked back and saw the woman's head poking through the hole. Turning around, Slocum chanced a quick scan of the horizon. His heart leaped when he saw a pennon fluttering in the wind at the head of a blue-clad column.

"The cavalry's on the way," he said. Slocum ducked when an Apache arrow sang past his head. He fired at the bowman, then went back to the hole. "We can hang on until they get here. They're not a mile off."

"I'll tell Arthur! He is so cynical." Mrs. Thornton dropped down and hurried to where her husband still fired fitfully at the Indians.

Slocum started to climb down, then saw that the soldiers were riding to the south, not coming to the ranch house. He couldn't believe that a frontal attack wouldn't

be best since nothing was gained taking the time to ride
long miles in a flanking maneuver. He jumped to his feet
and waved frantically.

"We're still here!" he shouted at the top of his lungs.
"Attack! Get them!" Slocum knew better than to remain
a target long and dropped to his knees as the air filled
with Apache bullets.

"What's wrong, Mr. Slocum?" asked the woman, her
head poking just above the roof again.

"They're not attacking. They're heading south. What's
in that direction?"

"Why, nothing. Open range. Our hands are down there
rounding up what few cattle we have left, but they aren't
in any danger. Arthur told them to hide if the Apaches
showed."

Slocum turned grim. He got to his feet again and fired
in the direction of the cavalry column, more in exasper-
ation than for any other reason. A bullet from a six-
shooter wouldn't carry that far, but he wanted to draw
their attention. How they could have missed the loud reports from so many gunshots was beyond him.

Unless . . . Garson was commanding the soldiers.

Slocum had assumed Cavendish would command the
rescue column himself, but the major might have been
absent from the fort. In that case, it would fall to Garson
to ride out.

And ignore them.

Slocum flopped belly-down and looked over the edge
of the roof, hunting for Dark Crow. If he could kill the
Apache chief, the rest of the renegades might leave. It
was a long shot but the only way Slocum could see that
any of them would get away alive.

He kept low and waited but never saw the Apache
chief. Firing twice wounded incautious braves but did
nothing to stop the hail of bullets turning the ranch house
into wormwood.

When both of his six-shooters came up empty, Slocum made his way back to the hole. He dropped heavily and had barely regained his balance, pain lancing all the way down his right leg, when Mrs. Thornton shoved two more six-guns into his hands.

"You'll have to use them," she said. "Arthur's not up to it."

"Tend your husband," Slocum said, seeing that Thornton lay on the floor. He was still conscious but white as a bleached sheet from loss of blood.

"There's nothing I can do," Mrs. Thornton said. "I'll keep your guns loaded as long as I can."

Slocum shot her a quick smile. He appreciated her gumption. Mrs. Thornton seemed a shy, reserved person, but underneath lay a core of steel. He fired four times as the door burst open and two Apaches tried to crowd inside. Slocum dropped them both, but one had held a torch.

He kicked the burning bundle out onto the porch, then saw it would still burn down the house unless he put it out. Slocum rushed forward, six-guns blazing. He kicked hard at the torch and sent it pinwheeling out into the yard.

Whether this was a trap set by Dark Crow, or the Indians were simply alert, Slocum didn't know. The arrows and bullets that came his way were intended to end his life. All that saved him was his game leg. As he kicked the torch away, he stepped down on his right leg and collapsed because it wouldn't hold his weight. Flopping around on his side, Slocum kept firing until he got back inside the house.

He looked up at Mrs. Thornton and said, "We're not getting out of here alive."

"I know," she said. "Perhaps I should see to Arthur." She handed him two more six-guns and then knelt by her husband.

Slocum sat on the floor, unable to stand. He fired occasionally but knew the majority of the Indians were circling to come up on the house from other sides. He could not see the Apaches creeping up on him, but he felt them. If the tables had been turned, that was exactly the kind of attack he would have made.

Slocum closed his eyes and listened to the incredible storm of bullets whining all around. But something seemed wrong to him. He swallowed his pain the best he could and looked outside.

"Soldiers," he said, not believing his eyes. "They're coming!"

He fired as the buffalo soldiers flushed the attacking Apaches, but he had no feeling that he even winged one of the Indians. It didn't matter. The soldiers routed the renegades in a matter of minutes.

Slocum pulled himself to his feet and hobbled onto the porch.

A black corporal rode up and saluted.

"Mr. Slocum, suh," the corporal said. "You and the Thorntons all right?"

"Barely," Slocum said. He looked around as a handful of buffalo soldiers returned and formed a squad behind the corporal. "Where's the rest of your company?"

The corporal looked a little anxious at this.

"Well, suh, it's like this. There ain't no officer with us. The lieutenant's on south of heah chasin' his own tail."

"Garson?" Slocum read the answer in the corporal's expression. "How'd you come to our rescue if your officer's not with you?"

"We was left behind at the fort. Seems Miz Washington saw what was happenin', might be she heard the lieutenant's orders to his company. So she talks it over with me. Me and her husband, we was good friends. Sergeant Washington was 'bout the best man I ever served with and—"

"And Maybelle convinced you to come out here on your own?"

"Reckon so. Miz Washington's a real persuasive woman."

"Damn," Slocum said in appreciation, sitting heavily on the porch railing. "This means you're going to be in hot water, doesn't it?"

"Been busted before. Ain't no disgrace. Why, Sergeant Washington got busted to private more'n once."

"What's your name, Corporal?" asked Slocum.

"What's the dif'rence?" the corporal said.

"I want to know who to thank for saving my life and those of the Thorntons."

The man smiled broadly, then saluted Slocum. "Corporal Donnelly, suh. At your service."

"Would you and your men like something to drink, Corporal?" asked Mrs. Thornton. "I don't have anything but water. I had some cider but I'm not sure what happened to it."

"Water'd be fine, ma'am," Donnelly said.

"Do you want to go after the Apaches?" Slocum asked. "That was Dark Crow leading them."

"Mr. Slocum, suh, we'd get ourselves chewed up and spit out if we tangled with more'n a couple Apaches. I counted at least a baker's dozen of them redskins."

Slocum stewed thinking how Lieutenant Garson had taken an entire company to the south. With that many men, Dark Crow would have fallen an easy prisoner.

The more he thought, the angrier he got.

"Suh, one of the privates found Sergeant Washington's horse. Or is that swayback ole refugee from a glue factory yours now?"

"Corporal Donnelly, that is about the most reliable horse I've ever ridden," Slocum said. "Pappy doesn't go fast, but he never stops. I've developed quite an affection for that habit."

"Just like you," Donnelly said, laughing. The corporal sobered and said, "I'll find a wagon and move them folks back to Mineral Springs so's they can be safer. Ain't right leavin' 'em out here so Dark Crow can come back."

"I don't want my house burned down!" complained Arthur Thornton. His wife had helped him from the ranch house to the steps. He waved around a six-gun with more determination than strength.

Slocum knew how the man felt. He was the same way.

"Mr. Thornton, your daughter's back in town and probably needs your help. Go see how Caroline's doing, then you can come back when your foreman and the rest of your cowhands round up your herd." This appealed to the man's sense of rightness. He nodded.

It took the better part of an hour to prepare the wagon with a mattress from the house for Arthur Thornton. His wife held his head as the wagon bumped and lurched along the road back to Mineral Springs. Slocum rode beside Corporal Donnelly.

"Think he's gonna make it?" the corporal asked.

"He's tough. I'm more worried about me getting to Fort Selden." Slocum's leg throbbed, and he felt every scratch and nick on his body.

"Yes, suh, you wouldn't want to die 'fore you got a chance to tell the lieutenant how you feel." Donnelly's wry sense of humor fit well with Slocum's mood.

"I'll need to reload before I talk to him."

This caused Donnelly, and several buffalo soldiers behind them who had been listening, to laugh. They didn't know Slocum wasn't joking.

After leaving the Thorntons in town with Caroline and Maybelle Washington, Slocum rode like the wind for Fort Selden. He trotted past the sentry and went directly to Major Cavendish's office. Standing outside was a lathered horse. Slocum hoped it belonged to the post commander because he was in no mood to get back in the saddle and track the man down.

"Oh, Mr. Slocum. Just the man I wanted to see," Cavendish said. He was unbuckling his gun belt and hanging it on a hook. "I've been to Fort Thorn again concerning the Apache problem. I—"

"Garson left the Thorntons to die at Dark Crow's hand. He had an entire company of men and rode past their ranch. The Apaches had the Thornton house surrounded and were shooting up the place, and Garson refused to come to their aid."

"What are you going on about?" Cavendish frowned.

Slocum explained all that had happened. The more he talked, the madder he got.

"Dereliction of duty is the least of his crimes," Slocum finished. He was ready to detail what he knew of Garson's gang of road agents when the door behind him opened.

"Major, I've returned from the sortie," Garson said.

Slocum spun, his hand going to the ebony butt of his six-gun.

"Slocum, don't," Cavendish said sharply. "I'll get to the bottom of this."

"What's going on, Major?" Garson fought to keep from smirking. The muscles in Slocum's arm twitched as he forced himself to leave his six-shooter where it was.

"Slocum says you rode past the Thornton ranch while it was being attacked by Dark Crow and his renegades."

"I was in the field, but I had no idea they were in trouble," Garson said insincerely. "I had heard of Apache raids to the south and took my company there."

"If Corporal Donnelly hadn't come to our rescue, Garson would have found nothing but arrow-filled corpses. Garson knew about the attack because Miss Thornton and Sergeant Washington's widow came to the fort to get soldiers out to the Thornton spread."

Garson shook his head and spread his hands as if he were totally innocent. "I can't say what tall tales hysterical women might pass along," the lieutenant said. "I was acting on scouting information." Then Garson's eyes narrowed. "Did you say Donnelly rode out to the ranch?"

"With a squad of men," Cavendish said. "You didn't send him?"

"No," Garson said sharply. "Donnelly was restricted to the fort for disciplinary reasons. I'm afraid he's acting more and more like Private Washington before he was put in the stockade."

"If you restricted him, that means he disobeyed direct orders."

"He saved three lives by doing his duty. That's more than I can say for Garson!" Slocum was furious now but saw the way the wind blew. Even if Caroline and Maybelle both told the major they had warned of the attack on the Thornton ranch, it would be their word against Garson's.

Maybelle's would be discounted out of hand as a grieving widow trying to get back at her husband's immediate superior. And Caroline? Slocum didn't know, but he figured Garson would come up with something. He had already planted the seed in Cavendish's mind that the women were probably hysterical.

"Mr. Slocum, I shall look into the matter, but it does not seem that Lieutenant Garson bears any responsibility for what happened at the Thornton ranch."

"Donnelly saved my life. I owe him."

"I'll discuss this matter further with Lieutenant Garson," Cavendish said, looking as if he had a mouthful of chili peppers and couldn't find a decent place to spit them out.

Slocum left without saying another word. Bringing the slippery Garson to justice was something he'd have to do, since it didn't appear the Army was ever going to have enough evidence against him. As he pushed past Garson, the lieutenant said in a whisper only Slocum could hear, "Ride on out, Slocum. Interfere again and you're a dead man!"

15

"I can't hold off an entire band of Apaches all alone," Slocum said. He mentioned Indians but meant road agents. "You need more than one shotgun guard on a wagon train."

"We intend to move fast," Horace Trevor said, mopping his face. The man tucked his sweat-dampened handkerchief into his coat pocket, drew out a dry one and continued the chore of soaking up all the perspiration. It was a lousy proposition, like guarding two supply wagons bound for Fort Selden and a stagecoach with only one guard: John Slocum.

"You could sprout wings and fly the supplies and still not avoid a determined band of renegades," Slocum said.

"You don't have to go, Slocum," Trevor said. "I won't hold it against you, since you're still recuperating from your leg injury. Won't hold it against any man wanting to avoid the danger."

"I'll do it," Slocum said, "but not if the stage is carrying money for the bank in Mineral Springs. That'd be too much temptation for any robber."

"No, not this time. Four passengers on their way north to Santa Fe, along with their gear. Nothing more. Not even mail."

"What are the supplies?" Slocum asked. He knew Fort Selden grew as much food locally as possible but had to bring in flour and other supplies from Texas.

"Barrels of nails, some food—bags of beans, I think."

"Nails?" Slocum shook his head. No supply wagon creaking under the weight of kegs of nails could hope to outrun an Apache. He pushed it out of his mind. If Dark Crow wanted to attack, no supply wagon could outrun his mounted warriors. Likewise, road agents owing their allegiance to Garson would never be outrun by a supply wagon, but the chance of Garson wanting to steal nails was next to nothing.

"Please, Slocum, matters are getting grave in Mineral Springs. We need the revenue, and shipments from Mesilla are being squeezed off."

"I said I'd do it."

Trevor gushed a bit more about how good an employee Slocum was. The only reason Slocum had agreed to ride along as guard was a small hope of tracking Garson's gang to their hideout. Slocum had not taken well to the diminutive lieutenant's threat. If he didn't flush the son of a bitch soon, Slocum intended to put an end to all threats coming from officers at Fort Selden—and that included Lieutenant Porter. Slocum had no proof they were in cahoots but thought it likely.

Slocum rode behind the stagecoach on its way south to Mesilla, where the driver and station master changed teams for the return trip. Watching carefully what was loaded onto the stage convinced Slocum that Trevor had not lied: Four passengers, all looking legitimate, and their luggage was all that got slung onto the top or into the canvas-covered boot at the back of the stage.

"Go on, roll out," Slocum called to the driver, a taciturn man who spat chewing tobacco and glared a lot. The entire way to Mesilla from Fort Selden he hadn't said three words. At the moment, that suited Slocum just fine. "I'll ride with the supply wagons."

"You're my guard," the driver complained.

"Don't go too fast, and we'll make it a wagon train," Slocum said. "The stage company's responsible for the freight wagons, too."

The driver spat tobacco, looked even more dour, then climbed into the driver's box and cracked the reins, getting his balky team pulling. He never looked back to see if his passengers were settled. From the shouts and frantic rattling around in the passenger compartment, it seemed he had caught at least one of the men by surprise.

Slocum knew the driver wouldn't rush, not in this heat. He wanted his team to keep pulling, and dead horses were worthless for that chore. The stagecoach rattled out of the Mesilla depot, leaving Slocum free to inspect the two freighters out back. The teamsters swore and kicked and got their mules hitched to the wagons.

Poking around under the canvas covering the load convinced Slocum that Horace Trevor had played straight with him. Nails, tools, even a few carefully packed plate glass windows, made up the bulk of the load. The rest was smaller items, possibly hardware to be used by the soldiers at the fort.

"You ready to ride?" one teamster growled at Slocum. Nobody was in a good mood, not that Slocum expected them to be. Driving in the heat of the day was crazy but safer than at night because it let them get a view of their surroundings.

Slocum motioned for the driver to pull out. The wagon creaked under the load and then rattled after the stage. In a few minutes, the second similarly laden wagon headed on the road for Mineral Springs and Fort Selden. Slocum pulled his hat brim down to shade his eyes and rode Pappy after the stage and the two wagons. He didn't mind eating their dust for a while since it gave him a chance to not only cover their back trail but also look to either side of the road to see if their passage was being noted by someone intent on robbery.

The hot day caused Slocum to drift a bit, but he was alert enough to notice two men in the distance when the supply wagons were less than ten miles outside Mineral Springs. He squinted and shaded his eyes with his hand to get a better view of the two riders. They were some distance off and did not signal anyone closer to the road. Slocum became more cautious and even edgy, wondering if they were lookouts posted by Garson. If so, they weren't doing their duty.

Or were they? Slocum had yet to figure out all the schemes Garson was mixed up in. The two riders let the wagons rumble on past, then rode down the far side of the ridge, where they watched.

Slocum rode up and alerted the two drivers, then got Pappy into a fast trot to overtake the stagecoach.

"What?" barked the driver, not bothering to slow as Slocum rode alongside.

"Two men were watching us mighty close," Slocum shouted over the rattle of the coach on the rocky, rough road. "You see any trouble brewing?"

"Nope." The driver spat and kept the team pulling at a steady clip.

Slocum checked the road behind, saw nothing, then galloped ahead to see if an ambush waited for the wagons. Again, he found nothing. The stagecoach veered off and went into Mineral Springs, a successful and safe run from Mesilla.

Trailing the two wagons, Slocum got more worried until they reached Fort Selden. The two riders might have been pilgrims on the trail heading somewhere else. They weren't Apaches from the little he could tell, but they might have been road agents. If so, they had not seen fit to hold up the supply wagons.

"I thought you were leaving the territory, Slocum," said Garson, coming from the post sutler's office. He carried a sheaf of papers.

"I decided I liked the desert, sidewinders and all," Slocum said.

"I'll talk to Trevor about paying you off so you can find greener pastures," Garson said. He pushed past Slocum and went to the rear of the first wagon. He made one check mark after another as he inventoried the supplies.

"Why isn't the post sutler doing that?" Slocum asked. The usual procedure was for a civilian supplier to sell the goods to the Army.

"He's busy and asked me to do it for him. I know what's due the fort." Garson glared at Slocum and started to say something more but a half dozen buffalo soldiers marched past. The lieutenant turned back to his inventory work, only to drop a few sheets of paper.

Quick as lightning, Slocum whipped out his knife and threw it, pinning the papers to the ground so they wouldn't blow away. He bent, pulled out his knife and glanced at the inventory Garson had taken.

Garson snatched the papers from Slocum.

"You checked in two dozen kegs of nails," Slocum said. "There aren't that many in the shipment."

"Not in this wagon. In both wagons there are."

"No, there's not," Slocum insisted. He had counted everything back in Mesilla and knew what freight had been moved along every dusty, burning hot inch of the way. He had estimated the weight in each wagon should it be necessary to outrun robbers. Slocum knew he had not misjudged the cargo so greatly.

"I say there are." Garson thrust out his jaw and put his hand on the butt of his revolver.

Slocum's mind flashed over the possibilities, then some of it came together for him. Garson checked in the supplies because he was shortchanging the post. The papers

might say two dozen kegs of nails had been delivered—
and paid for—but the reality of it was only half that were
actually delivered.

"Do you split the overcharges with the sutler?" Slocum
asked. "The Army's not getting what it's ordering. I suspect you're also not getting the quality, either."

"The Army has to put up with cheating sutlers all the
time," Garson said. "That's our lot in life."

Slocum started for Major Cavendish's office. Proof of
Garson's theft was apparent, but he had to be caught in
the act now, before he could change the orders and other
paperwork.

"He won't believe you, Slocum," called Garson. "This
is only half the order. I trust the sutler to ship the rest
later." Seeing this wasn't going to stop Slocum, the officer
added, "A shame about Corporal Donnelly, too."

"What?" Slocum spun, ready to gun the man down
where he stood smirking.

"Donnelly not only disobeys orders, why, I imagine he
is also stealing post supplies. He's working in the quar-
termaster corps since I restricted him to the post for in-
subordination. What he does with all the supplies he steals
is something I'd have to look into. Maybe he sells them
in Mineral Springs to unscrupulous civilians who sell
them back to the fort. Whatever that crook's doing with
post supplies, it's probably a hanging offense."

Slocum's fingers curled around the butt of his Colt
Navy. Shooting down Garson meant a world of trouble
for him, but it would remove a cancer growing in the
middle of Fort Selden.

"You won't shoot me. I'm not the only one who knows
Corporal Donnelly is a thief."

"Porter," said Slocum. "He's in cahoots with you."

"He's a fine and true fellow officer," corrected Garson.
"Now get the hell off the post before I have you shot."

"Try it," Slocum said, squaring off to face Garson.

"There's no need. I have a score of riflemen who will cut you down if you make a move for that hogleg." Garson sounded confident, but Slocum saw the man beginning to sweat now. A small tic appeared under the officer's eye, betraying the uncertainty he felt about Slocum's intentions.

Slocum almost drew, then realized killing Garson would only put Corporal Donnelly in the same stewpot that Benjamin Washington had been stirred into before being murdered. Garson and Porter ran Fort Selden and anyone crossing them ended up dead.

"Leave Donnelly out of it. The fight's between us."

"I'm no gunfighter," Garson said. "And I'm no fool, either!" He spun, putting his back to Slocum, then called out to the squad of buffalo soldiers marching back and forth across the parade ground, doing punishment duty, "Remove Mr. Slocum right away. All of you!"

Garson looked back over his shoulder. A cloud of anger turned his features ugly. "I can't seem to make you understand I mean business. Maybe you'll learn when Donnelly stands trial!"

Slocum half drew his Colt, then slid it back into the holster. He was no backshooter. And facing down a squad of soldiers ordered to remove him from Fort Selden wasn't going to solve any of the problems.

Slocum left, Garson's mocking laughter following him off the post.

16

"I can't believe Garson is doing this," Caroline Thornton said angrily. She stamped her foot. "You are going to get the corporal off on these trumped-up charges, aren't you, John?" She looked at him with her wide brown eyes, so trusting and sure he would turn the tide of military justice with only a few choice words.

Slocum was slow to answer. He had a plan brewing, and winning the woman's adulation was not part of it. If anything, he risked having her turn on him.

"I've got a few ideas," he told her truthfully. This was not good enough for Caroline. She had started to worm the details out of him when the fort trumpeter blew a long, ragged call to arms. From the direction of the mess hall came a clarion command for all parties to attend the court-martial immediately.

"Let's go," Caroline said, grabbing Slocum's arm and almost dragging him along. "The sooner you tell them what you know about that scoundrel Garson, the sooner the corporal will be freed."

Slocum had his own ax to grind with Garson. He had not forgotten Curt Degraff lying dead on the ground, a bullet in his back that Garson had intended for Slocum.

Garson had piled on one mockery of justice after another since then, killing Washington, the guards and the post doctor. Slocum wondered how long the lieutenant had been leading the band of road agents and terrorizing the entire countryside, from Fort Selden down to Mesilla. Worse than this, he had not been doing his duty and had let Dark Crow run free to cover the crimes he was committing.

There was not a whole lot about the lieutenant that Slocum liked. That made what he had to do all the more distasteful. But in the end, Garson would come to justice. Slocum would see to that.

"You take a seat up front, Mr. Slocum," Major Cavendish said. "You're one of the prime witnesses."

"See, John. I told you things would be just fine." Caroline scowled in Garson's direction, as if the officer cared what she thought. He was willing to let her and her family die at the hands of the Apaches rather than stop his own plundering for even a few minutes.

Caroline sat beside Slocum, whispering constantly about everything and everyone in the mess hall. Sweat poured down Slocum's face and caused his shirt to mat to his body. He wished the major had held Donnelly's court-martial after sundown when it was cooler, but he thought Cavendish wanted the disagreeable chore out of the way as quickly as possible so he could get back to his paperwork.

The charges were read by Lieutenant Porter, who showed some merriment at the notion one of the black soldiers was being railroaded. Slocum didn't know what role Porter had in Garson's schemes, but it might be considerable. After he dealt with Garson, he would poke around and see what could be done about Porter—and to hell with Major Cavendish's lack of officers to lead the buffalo soldiers in the field against the Apaches.

"I discovered the discrepancies in the tally when Mr.

Slocum there brought in a pair of supply wagons from Mesilla," Garson testified. He looked smugger by the minute. It took all of Slocum's willpower not to walk over and punch the arrogant bastard in the mouth. Instead, he kept a poker face and listened carefully to every lie Garson told.

"Thank you, Lieutenant. Please stand down. The court calls John Slocum."

"Go on, John. Tell them what really happened!" urged Caroline, barely able to sit still on the hard bench.

Slocum looked at Donnelly sitting at the other side of the room. The corporal flashed him a weak smile. Slocum felt like a traitor as he was sworn in and faced the major.

"Tell us what you observed, Mr. Slocum," Cavendish said. The major had his pencil ready to take notes. Slocum was going to make it easy for him.

"Everything the lieutenant said is pretty much the way I saw it," Slocum said.

A hush fell over the mess hall. Then everyone began shouting and talking at the same time, forcing Cavendish to rap for silence.

"How's that again?" Cavendish asked. "I thought you had accused someone else of stealing the supplies." The major shot a quick look at Garson, who sat nearby with a grin on his face.

"Reckon a man can be wrong. Lieutenant Garson tallied the cargo brought up from Mesilla, and since it matched when we left, that means someone at Fort Selden did the stealing. The only one who might have done that is Corporal Donnelly."

The buffalo soldiers shot to their feet, angrily shouting at Slocum. The major used the butt of his revolver to gavel them to silence.

"So, you think Corporal Donnelly is the thief?"

"Who else could it be?"

Slocum looked at Caroline, who sat with her mouth

gaping in astonishment. It was hard watching her react to his words, but it was harder forcing himself to look at the corporal. The man sat looking as stunned as if someone had laid a heavy plank alongside his head. Then Donnelly's expression changed to one of resignation. The buffalo soldiers had been at the utter bottom of the chain of command for so long, no indignity was unexpected. Donnelly turned stoic in the face of such injustice. Slocum watched as Donnelly's jaw firmed and he sat straighter, ready for whatever punishment the major decided on.

"This is unusual," Cavendish said carefully. "There were not sufficient officers for a proper court-martial, but now that we have two witnesses—Corporal Donnelly's immediate superior and a civilian who has performed well for us as both a hunter and a scout—there is little need to continue."

"I protest!" Caroline leaped to her feet. "He's innocent. You can't convict him on the say-so of these . . . these . . . men!" She was so beside herself with rage she sputtered.

"How do you plead, Corporal?" asked Cavendish, ignoring Caroline's outburst.

"You know what's right, Major," Donnelly said, getting to his feet and standing at attention. "I don't reckon there's nuthin' I can add that'll change anything."

"I suppose not," Cavendish said, staring at Slocum. He shuffled the papers in front of him, then said in a loud voice, "This court finds you guilty as charged on the count of theft of Army property. You are reduced in rank and sentenced to six months in the stockade at hard labor. At the time of completion of your sentence, you will be dishonorably discharged from the U.S. Army."

A new tumult broke over the assembled soldiers in the mess hall.

Loud enough to drown out the roar, Major Cavendish said, "Take the prisoner away. The rest of you, dismissed!"

Slocum sat on the witness chair where he had ridden out the storm of protest over his testimony. Caroline shot him a hot look that would have melted steel, then turned and hurried off to get a word with Donnelly before they locked him up.

Garson and Porter sauntered over to Slocum, looked around to be certain no one could overhear, then Garson said, "That was quite a surprise, Slocum."

Slocum only shrugged. He waited for what he knew would come next.

"Do you think we might have misjudged him?" Garson said to Porter, as if Slocum had ceased to exist.

"Might have, might have," Porter answered.

"Why'd you change your mind about what really happened?" Garson asked.

"I didn't change my mind. You're as guilty as sin. You're stealing by shortchanging the army, you and the sutler."

"Doesn't sound like he's changed his tune at all," Porter said, resting his hand on the butt of his six-shooter.

"I changed my mind, that's all," Slocum said. "You can take anything you want from the post and not get caught at it. That means you're getting rich." Slocum made a point of looking around the now empty mess hall. "Who else at Fort Selden is getting rich?"

"Are you saying you might want in on the action?" asked Porter. He looked at Garson and shook his head. "Don't fall for it. He's trying to get us to—"

"I know you're stealing from the fort, and I know you're the leader of the gang of outlaws robbing the stage. I suppose there's even more I don't know about." Slocum swallowed bile as it rose in his throat. He knew he could not mention Curt Degraff without giving himself away. "I don't need to get evidence on you. I already know what's going on, and I'd surely like to get a share of it."

"Would you now, Slocum?" Garson asked thoughtfully.

"Might be we have a place for a man of your abilities. You look as if you can use that hogleg pretty well."

"I'm fast enough to stay alive," Slocum said. "And I always hit what I aim for."

"You got a head on your shoulders, too," Garson said. "You don't panic easy."

Slocum let the two officers work it out between themselves. Porter argued against telling Slocum any more, but Garson seemed intrigued with the idea of turning a former foe into an ally. They turned back to him.

"We need an inside man at the stage company, one who knows when shipments to the bank are being made."

"From the way you hit the shipments of greenbacks so regular-like, I figured you already had someone telling you."

"Turns out, he got spooked and hightailed it. He was the station master down in Mesilla. That leaves us with a potentially lucrative source of money slipping away unless we change that. You and Trevor are hitting it off."

"I know when the shipments are," Slocum said.

"Excellent. Then we can do business. Very profitable business," Garson said. "You tell us when the next shipment to the Mineral Springs bank is, and we'll take it from there."

"I might be riding shotgun," Slocum said.

"Even better," Garson said.

"It won't get sloppy like the last stage holdup," Porter said, coming around to agreeing with Garson. It was obvious which of them was the boss.

"How'd the driver and the passenger get away like that?" Slocum asked.

"It doesn't matter," Garson said sharply. "The Apaches finished the job for us. We want it to look like they're doing the thieving anyway. So, are you in?" Garson eyed Slocum like a vulture eyes a man dying in the desert.

"I'm in," Slocum said. "On one condition."

Both Garson and Porter tensed. Garson asked, "What's that?"

"I get ten percent of the loot."

Garson laughed loudly, then thrust out his hand for Slocum to shake.

"A deal!" Garson cried.

Slocum shook hands and wanted to wash his off right away. But he was in the gang.

17

"There's nothing to it," Garson said to Slocum. "All you need do is pass the word along when you hear of a big shipment coming."

"Greenbacks?" Slocum asked warily. He saw the glint in Garson's eye and knew the lieutenant wanted something more than a handful of paper that was well nigh useless outside New Mexico Territory.

"Gold, coins, silver—I want metal now," Garson said, not even trying to hide his greed. "You get the lion's share. You knew there were quite a few of us in the gang when you asked for a tenth, didn't you?"

Slocum only nodded. He had guessed at how many were in the gang. Garson had now as much as told him there were more than ten.

"It'll be worth giving you a bigger cut than even Porter gets, if you can deliver."

"Why does Porter get a bigger cut?" asked Slocum. "He's not the boss. You are."

Garson turned colder. "Don't forget it, either," the officer said curtly. "He's my right-hand man. Saved my life a couple times. I owe him, so he rakes in a double share."

"So he gets the same cut as you?"

"Don't go getting too nosy," Garson said in a tone that told Slocum not to probe anymore. "All you need to do is tell me when some specie'll be shipped up the road from the south."

Slocum nodded, then said, "It's good to see something coming out of my stay here. You've got a corner on all the action—except what Dark Crow dishes out."

"Don't worry about the Apaches," Garson said. "They've got a hidden camp, and I keep a close watch on them. I know every move they make."

Slocum went cold inside. Garson could have captured the renegade chief at any time if this were true—and it had the ring of sincerity to it. This was another black mark against Garson and his thieving, murdering ways.

"I'd better get on back to Mineral Springs and see what Trevor has to say."

"You do that." Garson did a snappy about-face and marched off to talk to Porter. The two men looked back in Slocum's direction, but he tried to pretend he didn't notice. Slocum seethed inside at what he had to do. Riding out of Fort Selden with Caroline looking daggers at him was about the hardest thing he ever had to do.

Except knowing he had testified to send Donnelly to the stockade for six months of hard labor in the murderously hot New Mexico sun.

Slocum rode Pappy toward Mineral Springs but cut off the road as quickly as he could once he was out of sight of the fort. He settled down to wait once more. He'd had poor luck before tracking Garson when he left the post, but then the outlaw had been with an entire squad of buffalo soldiers and Slocum had had one of the worst runs of bad luck he'd ever experienced.

Thinking about how he had almost been hanged and shot by the guard above Garson's camp set his leg to throbbing. Even as it ached and made him increasingly uncomfortable, Slocum realized his luck had not been all bad. He had survived—and he would see Garson pay for killing Degraff and all the other crimes. It was a pity he had to send Donnelly to the stockade to get the evidence he needed.

Slocum heard the sound of hooves a little after sundown and hurried to a vantage point near the road in time to see a buffalo soldier urging a tired, broken-down nag to greater speed. Slocum recognized Private Farmer as one of the men in Donnelly's squad. He had to smile at the trouble Farmer was having. The more the soldier tried to get speed from the horse, the more resolute the horse became to keep plodding along at the same leisurely gait.

The soldier passed slowly on his way toward Mineral Springs, grumbling as he rode.

Farmer had barely ridden out of sight when Slocum heard a steadier clop of horse's hooves.

"Pay dirt!" Slocum exclaimed, then fell silent as Garson trotted along the road. This time he did not ride at the head of a company of buffalo soldiers. From the way his head swiveled around, looking in all directions, he obviously worried someone might see him. Slocum froze where he stood, not even daring to breathe until Garson passed his hiding place.

When the officer vanished down the road, Slocum hurried back to Pappy and swung into the saddle. The horse turned a head in his direction and looked accusingly at him. Slocum had no time to let the horse crop at the dry grass and got the swaybacked animal moving. For about a quarter mile Slocum rode a dozen yards off the dirt track leading to Mineral Springs, then cut across the sandy stretch when he no longer got much in the way of cover from the vegetation and relied on his sharp senses to keep from coming up on Garson in the dark.

He heard the steady clip-clop of a horse ahead. The gait was different from Farmer's horse. Slocum wanted to locate the camp where Garson's gang hid out because he thought the diminutive officer might have hidden near it all the loot he had stolen. Find the stolen money and Slocum had a strong case against Garson, even if it looked as if he might have to gun the man down himself.

Slocum had done worse in his day and had more than a couple wanted posters following him because of it. But this time he wanted Garson brought to public justice to show the soldiers at Fort Selden that Washington's death was not the savage act of Apaches. More than this, seeing the rope fastened around Garson's neck before the gallows trapdoor opened would go a long way to evening the score for backshooting Degraff.

Slocum slowed and finally dismounted to study the dry ground. A half moon rose to give him enough silvery light to study the tracks and determine that Garson had left the road, heading south—in the same direction he had gone during Dark Crow's attack on the Thorntons at their ranch house. Something on the Thornton spread drew Garson.

His treasure hoard? Slocum hoped so.

He could not see the officer ahead of him, but the desert was rockier here and ridges cut through the land, making both travel and observation difficult. That made it easier for Slocum to trail Garson, but it also presented a danger. He might ride up on the officer and never know it until it was too late. To counter any questions Garson might have in such a case, Slocum began going over a dozen different stories explaining his reason for being out on the desert at night—and on Garson's trail.

Slocum was so deep in thought trying to come up with the perfect lie that the gunshot startled him. His hand flashed to his holstered six-gun, but he did not draw. The shot had come from behind him, not ahead, and there had been no whistle of hot lead passing close to him. If Garson had tried to ambush him, the shot wouldn't have missed.

A second gunshot decided Slocum. As much as he wanted to find Garson's plunder, he had to investigate the gunshots. Dark Crow still roamed the land, although what the Apache chief would be doing out after sundown was beyond him. Superstition—and even legitimate fear of rattlers—kept the Apaches close to their camps at night.

Slocum got back to the road leading to Mineral Springs and put his heels to Pappy's flanks. The horse dutifully picked up the pace but Slocum soon saw he wasn't going to get more than a trot out of the old horse. Chafing at the slow but steady pace, Slocum prepared himself for the worst. Garson's gang might be active tonight.

When he came to a horse lying beside the road, Slocum dismounted and quickly looked over the dead animal. Two shots had ended its life. Further examination of the faint hoofprints showed how the horse had strayed off the sunbaked dirt ruts and had stepped in a prairie dog hole near the road. Slocum got back on his horse and picked up the pace again, trotting along the road to overtake the soldier he had seen. While he could not be sure, Slocum thought this was Private Farmer's horse.

After a few minutes, Slocum failed to find the buffalo soldier. More curious than worried, Slocum wheeled around, wondering if Farmer had started walking back to Fort Selden. He rode ten minutes and still didn't find the soldier. Slocum's curiosity turned to concern for the man's safety. The evidence surrounding the dead horse and the two gunshots showed nothing untoward had happened other than the horse breaking its leg, but where had Farmer gone? He had not continued along the road to Mineral Springs, nor had he returned to the cavalry post. Leaving the road only led into desert. Slocum knew the lay of the land well enough to know Farmer wasn't following a shortcut to either town or Fort Selden.

He might be going to the distant Rio Grande to get water, but Slocum doubted it. Town was closer, if the soldier had developed a thirst.

Finding the carcass again, Slocum carefully circled the

dead horse until he found faint signs that Farmer had trudged off into the desert. The single line of footprints belied any danger to the soldier, but Slocum had to find out. He followed on foot, much to Pappy's relief. It took the better part of a half hour before Slocum spotted Private Farmer. The buffalo soldier had his saddle slung over his shoulder and his rifle in the other hand as he tramped along. The night wind blowing across the desert caught and carried snippets of the man's steady cursing.

Slocum mounted and rode down a steep slope, careful of how he approached Farmer. The man held a Spencer and might be inclined to use it if someone startled him by coming out of the darkness unexpectedly.

"Private!" Slocum yelled when he got to a level stretch. Farmer was about twenty yards off. The man dropped his saddle and whirled around, clutching his rifle with both hands. "Farmer! Hey, Farmer! It's me, Slocum. You in trouble?"

"Git on out of heah," Farmer shouted. He lifted the rifle and aimed it at Slocum. "You done ruint Donnelly. You ain't gonna ruin me!"

Slocum had no time or inclination to explain why he had so swiftly testified against the corporal.

"I don't want to do a danged thing to you," Slocum said, exasperated now. Farmer was not hurt and Slocum had abandoned Garson's trail to find this out. He would have to come up with some other scheme to locate Garson's hidden loot, and this only prolonged Donnelly's stay in the stockade.

"You ain't takin' me back. I won't go!"

Slocum hesitated now, trying to make sense out of what Farmer was shouting. The fright in the man's voice struck Slocum as misplaced, even if the soldier worried over Donnelly's fate.

"What's going on?" Slocum asked. He made no move for his Colt Navy. That would have set off Farmer and brought a hail of .50-caliber slugs from the rifle. "Are you running from someone?"

"I'm quittin'! I cain't take no moah!"

"Quitting? You mean you're deserting?"

"You cain't take me back. I won't go! I thought you was he'pin' Miss Thornton, but you testified 'gainst Donnelly. You're one of them!"

"I'm not," Slocum said. "And I'm not here to take you back. Mind if I smoke?" He rode closer, got off Pappy and slowly pulled the makings from his shirt pocket. He rolled a cigarette, then held out the tobacco and papers for Farmer. The soldier couldn't roll a smoke and hold the rifle on him at the same time.

Slocum lit his cigarette about the time Farmer lowered his rifle and took the offered tobacco pouch. Farmer expertly fixed his own and let Slocum light the tip from the coal on his cigarette.

"This shore do taste mighty fine," Farmer said, his head in a cloud of blue smoke as he puffed away.

"You want to tell me what's going on?" Slocum asked. "Is it something Garson did?"

"Garson, Porter, you—the whole danged lot," Farmer said gloomily. "No white folks at the post treat us decent. We might as well have stayed slaves."

"You don't believe that," Slocum said, smoking more slowly. Farmer was almost done with his. Slocum silently indicated Farmer ought to roll himself another.

"Shore 'nuff. Look at what you done to Donnelly. He didn't steal nuthin' and you know it."

"They'll come after you if you desert," Slocum said, remembering Benjamin Washington and his reason for leaving the post. "If they don't stand you in front of a firing squad, they'll put you in jail for the rest of your life."

"I cain't take it no moah," Farmer said plaintively.

"Is that what Sergeant Washington would have said?"

asked Slocum. "Given the chance, do you think Corporal Donnelly would turn tail and run? Anything the officers say about you will be true if you desert."

"I dunno."

"How many have deserted from Fort Selden?"

"I . . . I don't know. Not many," Farmer said, turning sullen.

"None. The Negro companies in the army have the lowest desertion rate. It wouldn't surprise me if you don't win the most medals, too," Slocum said.

"We done our share. But they cain't ask me to do no moah!"

"How long until your hitch is up?" Slocum asked.

"A year," Farmer said. He finished his cigarette and carefully ground it out and spread the precious few shards of tobacco all around so no one trailing him could find a trace. The soldier realized what he was doing and looked sheepish now. "Sergeant Washington, he done taught me to do this. Go through the land and not disturb so much as a leaf, not that there are many leaves in this heah desert."

"You haven't deserted yet," Slocum said. "Not until you fail to show up at reveille."

"Reckon that's so," Farmer allowed. "You sayin' you won't turn me in if'n I go back now?"

"There's no crime to turn you in for," Slocum said.

"Thass so," Farmer said, working up his gumption to return to Fort Selden. "But I done kilt my horse. I stole that mare, and she upped and broke a leg."

"I saw that," Slocum said. "Might be that the major owes me a horse."

"You got the sergeant's. Pappy's a right good horse," Farmer said in some admiration, ignoring the swayed back, sad eyes and scraggly tail.

"Let's you and me ride back to Fort Selden. We can

work out the problem with the horse. Might be that no one even noticed the horse is gone."

"Wasn't my usual horse. Don't know who rides that mare."

Slocum knew Farmer would punish himself more—and Cavendish would get better soldiering from Farmer—over the next year of his enlistment than any court-martial could mete out.

They rode together until they got into sight of Fort Selden.

"Why don't you get on back? I'll follow," Slocum said.

"You distract them boys at the gate," Farmer said. "They ain't too bright, but they got good eyes." The private slipped away into the darkness, leaving Slocum astride Pappy a hundred yards from the gate where two sentries dozed. Slocum rode forward slowly, giving Farmer time to get over the low wall and back to his barracks.

Slocum had hardly reached the gate when a ruckus went up inside the fort. Gunshots brought the entire company rushing out, half-dressed and the officers carrying sabers or pistols.

"What's going on?" demanded Major Cavendish, rubbing sleep from his eyes. He swung the heavy saber around, as if warding off legions of unseen Apache fighters.

"I found him sneaking back in," Lieutenant Porter said, holding Farmer by the scruff of the neck.

"He was with me," Slocum said, trying to find an excuse that would let them all go away happy. He saw in a flash this was the wrong thing to say. Porter's face lit up as he dragged Farmer forward and threw him to his knees in front of the major.

"There it is, sir. Slocum brought back a deserter. Here he is!"

"He didn't desert," Slocum started, but was cut off by Porter pressing the muzzle of his six-shooter behind Farmer's ear. The expression on the officer's face made it clear what would happen if Slocum said another world. Porter would gleefully kill Farmer.

He and Garson were cut from the same cloth.

"You brought us a deserter, Slocum?" asked Cavendish, still groggy from sleep.

Slocum said nothing as Porter cocked the six-gun. The lieutenant dared him to deny it, but that didn't mean Slocum had to agree to it.

"He did, sir. As I am officer of the watch, Slocum reported straight away to me with the private. Shall I put him in the stockade?"

"Mr. Slocum, suh, you—" Farmer looked up at him with pleading eyes. Then the private's resolve hardened— as did his attitude toward Slocum and every other white man. He didn't realize Slocum's silence kept him from getting his head blown off then and there.

"Take him to the stockade," ordered Porter, "but don't put him in the same cell as Donnelly. Keep them apart. We wouldn't want them conspiring to escape."

Slocum knew the last was for his ears only. It was a veiled threat. If he tried to cross Garson and Porter, both Donnelly and Farmer would die in a fake escape attempt. They had already shown by killing Washington and his guards that no one was safe on the post.

Slocum looked around the tight circle of black soldiers in the parade ground. He saw nothing but smoldering hatred for him in their eyes. And he couldn't blame them.

18

Slocum had faced men intent on killing him but never had he faced such fury as he did now. Caroline Thornton glared at him, her jaw set firmly and her brown eyes flashing angrily.

"I heard what happened last night at the fort," she said, her voice husky with anger. "How could you?"

"I suppose you're talking about Private Farmer," he said. Word had spread fast, but he had not thought Caroline would hear about it for a while yet. But she saw Maybelle Washington regularly and might have learned from her all that had happened.

"You know I am, Mr. Slocum," Caroline said hotly. "You turned him in! You could have sneaked him back in. He was trying to do the right thing, and you turned him over to that odious Lieutenant Porter!"

"I did what I had to," Slocum said, looking past the furious woman to where Garson and three rough-looking men stood across Mineral Springs' main street. He wanted to explain everything to Caroline but couldn't with Garson watching so closely. Slocum didn't trust the man but had to play along, at least for a little while longer.

"I trusted you. How could I have been so blind?"

Slocum started to say something, but Caroline slapped him hard enough to sting. She reared back like she was going to slap him again, stopped and stalked off, head held high.

"Looks like the little filly and you aren't getting along anymore," Garson said. The other three men had stayed across the street, trying to look inconspicuous. In a town as small as Mineral Springs, any strangers stood out. However, no one paid them any mind today and they huddled together in a short alley alongside the bakery.

"Trevor called me to his office," Slocum said. "There's something in the wind by the way he was acting."

"Big?" Garson got a sly look in his eye.

"Real big," Slocum agreed.

"Don't let me keep you from your job," Garson said. "You hie on over there and find out what Mr. Trevor wants." Garson crossed the street to the trio of men, spoke briefly and then left them. Slocum had the feeling the three were spying on him. Although he could not identify them as being members of Garson's gang of road agents, he didn't doubt that was exactly who they were.

He walked slowly to the stagecoach office, rubbing his cheek where Caroline had slapped it. Somehow, it stung more now than when she had laid those long fingers of hers across his face.

"Slocum, come on in. Shut the door. We've got to hurry. There's no time, no time," Horace Trevor said, bustling about like an ant who couldn't find his hill.

"What's in the wind?"

"Gold, a big gold shipment from Mesilla. About the biggest this town's ever seen, and it's due here at the end of the week. I need you to ride south and then escort the stage back."

"Ride guard? How many others?"

"Just you. We want this to seem like an ordinary shipment, nothing unusual, just more mail and worthless things like that."

"You're trying to sneak it past the road agents," Slocum said, half accusingly. Such a tactic was worthless, and the station master ought to know that.

"It's risky, I know, but I've been told to do this by my boss in El Paso. The gold's bound for Fort Union. No reason to leave that much here in Mineral Springs." Trevor said, almost to himself.

Slocum looked out the window of the depot and saw Garson's men across the street, watching like vultures waiting for something weak to die.

"Count on me," Slocum said. Then he left to tell Garson what he had been told.

"You're mighty edgy," Slocum said to the stagecoach driver as they climbed into the box. Slocum dropped, resting his rifle against the side. The coach rocked as the passengers got in and slammed the compartment door behind them.

"I got a right to be as nervy as a rotten tooth," the driver said. "You know what we're carryin'?"

Slocum put his foot on the strongbox and scooted over so the man could take the long whip from its holder.

"Reckon I do," Slocum said.

"We got Apaches scalpin' men and women and children," the driver said, snapping the whip tentatively. The team shied a little, but the man held them in control. "Them Injuns ain't the worst, either. We got road agents workin' this trail that are mean and nasty and as likely to shoot you as look at you." He reared back and sent the long black whip snaking out to snap like a firecracker directly over the lead horse's head. The horse got to pulling, and the driver took all the reins in both hands to control the spirited team.

"All that's true," Slocum said, "but the cavalry'll take care of them all."

"I hope so," the driver said. "I'd as soon see it happen *after* we'd reached Albuquerque, though. I ain't no hero." The driver looked sidelong at Slocum, spat and then asked, "Are you?"

"I'm not a hero," Slocum said.

"Good. I hate heroes. All I want is a shotgun messenger who wants to get drunk at the end of the day. I can understand that."

The choking dust from the road forced Slocum to pull up his bandanna so he looked more like a highwayman than Garson was likely to. Slocum had told Garson the details of the gold shipment, but the lieutenant had not bothered to tell Slocum where the gang was going to stop the stage. Garson had told Slocum to take care of the driver and make certain none of the passengers drew six-shooters and opened fire when the gang stopped the stage. Otherwise, the gang would do it all.

Garson had told Slocum they would split the gold then and there so Slocum could go his way, a fortune riding in his saddlebags.

Somehow, Slocum doubted that was Garson's real plan. Leaving witnesses had never been part of the way he and his band of cutthroats worked.

Slocum intended to stay alert, but the rolling motion of the coach lulled him to sleep. Besides, riding with his eyes closed kept the grit and sand out of them. He snapped fully awake when the driver began cussing a blue streak.

"What's wrong?" Slocum asked. Then he saw the problem. Masked men blocked the road.

"You wantin' to shoot it out with them?" the driver asked. Then he answered his own question. "I sure as hell don't."

"Good idea," Slocum said. He lifted his rifle, made sure his Colt Navy was close at hand, then felt the outline of a derringer in his vest pocket. He was armed and ready for anything that might happen. "Go along with me," Slocum told the driver as he poked his rifle into the man's ribs.

"You! You're one of them devils!" The driver sounded outraged, but his face was a mask of fear.

"Stop the stage," Slocum said. Louder, so his words would carry to the road agents ahead, he said, "Stop or I'll plug you!" He fired his rifle, the bullet missing the driver by a foot or more.

This caused the driver to rear back and tug hard on the reins. Then he put his foot on the brake and shoved hard on it. The stagecoach skidded slightly in the dirt and then came to a halt less than ten yards from where Garson's gang waited.

"You've done well, Slocum," a masked Garson said, riding up. "You stupid son of a bitch!" Garson pointed his drawn six-gun directly at Slocum. "Drop the rifle and lose that smoke wagon. Now!"

"Reckon you done stepped in it," the driver muttered. Slocum ignored the driver's comment as he dropped both his rifle and Colt Navy.

"Get down," Garson said.

Slocum jumped over, stepped onto the wheel and dropped to the ground. As he turned away from Garson, he slipped the derringer from his pocket and held it hidden in his hand.

"You're the stupid one, Garson," Slocum said. "You and Porter. You're throwing away your careers with this petty thieving."

"Petty? There's a thousand dollars in gold coin in that box." Garson pulled down his mask and waved his hand. "Get the box, Porter. I want to see the gold sparkling in the sunlight!"

Porter dismounted and got into the driver's box. He

fumbled a minute, then said, "The strongbox is chained down."

"Shoot off the lock," Garson said irritably. He waved to the other men and had them circle the stagecoach so no one could get away.

"You learned your lesson, didn't you?" asked Slocum.

"What are you going on about?"

"The driver and a passenger got away from the last stage you robbed. You're not taking a chance this time."

"That was Porter's doing," Garson said. "I had to be on patrol then."

"How many times have you robbed a stage?" Slocum asked. "Why weren't you satisfied with the money you stole from the post supplies?"

"That was chicken feed," Garson said. "I had to split the money with the sutler. By the time I paid shares to the gang, there wasn't much. That's when I hit on the idea of adding stagecoach robbery to my way of getting enough spending money."

"You and Porter," Slocum said, shaking his head. "Any others at Fort Selden?"

"You talk too damned much, but if that's the way you want to spend your last minutes alive, then ramble on, Slocum. I figure we'll line the lot of you up and shoot you, then scalp you. Another Apache raid. What a goddamn shame!" Garson laughed harshly.

Porter shot twice, then heaved the strongbox out. It hit the ground and broke open.

"Lookee there," said the driver, eyes wide as he stared at the contents as they spilled out. "That's nothin' but worthless rock!"

"What?" Both Garson and Porter pawed through the rocks and saw the driver was right. Garson looked up and shoved his gun at Slocum. "Where's the gold?"

"Might be I stole it already and hid it," Slocum said. "Might be I didn't trust you."

"You son of a bitch!" Garson cocked his six-shooter and started to shoot Slocum.

"Wait," Porter cried. "Kill him and we'll never get the gold."

"He won't tell us, no matter what we do to him," Garson said, reading Slocum right. "Kill him. Kill the passengers and let's get the hell out of here."

"Aren't you even going to ask the passengers to get out?" Slocum's palm sweat as he clutched the tiny two-shot pistol. He would die if Garson squeezed the trigger on his six-shooter. Slocum needed a chance to bring the tiny popgun into play.

"Get 'em out," ordered Garson. "Get them all out. I want Slocum to watch each and every one of them being gunned down so that'll be the last thing on his mind."

The door to the compartment opened and two men jumped down. One turned and spoke to the third man still inside. "We've heard enough, sir."

"What are you talking about?" demanded Garson.

"I'm a federal marshal," the taller of the two said, moving his coat back to show the badge on his vest. "This here gent is my deputy. But we won't be arresting you. Now those other gents in your gang, the ones not in the Army, their asses are mine!"

"I don't understand what's going on," complained Porter.

"Shoot them!" ordered Garson.

"Halt!" came the sharp command from inside the compartment. Major Cavendish swung out. "The reason Marshal Hendrix doesn't want you, Garson, is that you're my prisoner. I hereby place you under arrest."

"Cavendish?" Garson looked at Slocum and then laughed. "You think I'm going to obey this stuffed shirt? That I'm going to let him take me back to Fort Selden to be hanged?"

"Hang or die on the spot," Cavendish said coldly. "Look around you."

Garson jerked around and saw the cordon of buffalo soldiers. His eyes went wide when he saw Corporal Donnelly at the head of one squad.

"The corporal is a good soldier and won't shoot you, as much as he wants to, unless I order him to do so." Cavendish had not expected Garson's next move. But Slocum had.

Moving like a striking snake, Slocum batted Garson's six-shooter to one side. The pistol discharged before its bullet could end Donnelly's life. Then Slocum shoved his derringer into the side of Garson's throat.

"Move a muscle and you're dead," Slocum growled. He wanted Garson to struggle, to put up a fight. He wanted to kill Garson because he had backshot Curt Degraff, had murdered Washington and committed so many other crimes that Slocum got dizzy thinking about them.

"Slocum," came a quiet voice. "Mr. Slocum. You don't have to cover him any longer. He has given up."

Major Cavendish pulled away Slocum's hand holding the derringer. Garson sobbed and fell to his knees as the blue-coated buffalo soldiers grabbed him. The rest of the gang, including Lieutenant Porter, had already been hogtied.

"I know you want to kill him, Mr. Slocum, but don't. Leave that to the court-martial. Trust in justice."

Reluctantly, Slocum backed off.

"I want to be at the execution," he said.

"Unless I miss my guess, a lot of people will want to be there." Cavendish said.

The streets of Mineral Springs bustled with more activity than Slocum had ever seen. Marshal Hendrix had brought in a small posse from El Paso to take custody of the civilians in Garson's gang. In addition to the deputies, a full company of buffalo soldiers remained to guard Garson and Porter in the town's small calaboose.

"It's more like a circus than anything I've seen in years," Horace Trevor said. "I am glad everything worked out. I could not stand having another driver killed." The station master wiped at a forehead beaded with sweat.

"Thanks for arranging with Cavendish to have the federal marshal on the stage, too," Slocum said. Because of the way Garson's men had dogged his every step, he had been unable to get word to Cavendish after setting up the trap with the Fort Selden commander. Things had worked out well, even to Slocum getting a small reward for the capture of the road agents.

"You had everything arranged. It was easy, easy I say," Trevor went on. "Do you think they'll take them all to prison soon?"

"Garson stands trial in a few days," came a soft voice from the doorway. Slocum looked over his shoulder to see Caroline Thornton standing there, outlined by the bright sun outside. It made her soft brown hair turn golden like an angel's halo. "So you lied to me," she said to Slocum with mock severity.

"He had to, Miss Thornton," Trevor babbled. "There was no way he could risk you getting involved. He talked Major Cavendish into setting the trap."

"Why did you testify against Corporal Donnelly?" she asked Slocum point-blank.

"Garson wanted to try him for Washington's murder. The way things were at Fort Selden, he could have found enough people to lie and convict him. By convicting Donnelly on the trumped-up theft charges, Garson felt he had won. That gave me a way of throwing in with him."

"Or pretending to do so to trap him," Caroline said.

"Yes, yes, Mr. Slocum was quite adroit at that. He convinced the major to go along." Trevor looked more and more uncomfortable because he was being ignored as Slocum and Caroline spoke.

"He knew Donnelly wasn't guilty," Slocum told Caroline. "He knew my feelings about Garson and how I was likely to shoot him down for killing Degraff. But I had no proof."

"Cavendish had to see for himself," Caroline said. "That's why he rode in the stage. What if Garson hadn't been there with his gang? What if the soldiers hadn't been nearby when Garson did hold up the stage? You'd all have been killed."

"Garson was too greedy. I made out the shipment as being huge, too huge for him to trust to his gang—or even his partner, Porter. As to Donnelly having the soldiers at the right place, that was about where the other stage had been ambushed. I reckoned Garson was comfortable there."

"And if he had robbed the stage somewhere else?" Caroline pressed. She moved across the room and stood close to Slocum, looking up at him. Adoration had replaced contempt in her brown eyes.

"The road agents would have had a big fight on their hands," Slocum said. "Marshal Hendrix and his deputy had shotguns and a case of shells between them. Major Cavendish had two six-shooters and a pocketful of ammo."

"You could have been killed," Caroline said.

"The corporal would have heard the gunfire and come running," Slocum said. "The big risk we took was Garson or someone in his gang seeing an entire company of soldiers and figuring out they were riding into a trap."

"You did this all to avenge Benjamin Washington." Caroline said, moving even closer. Her breasts rubbed into Slocum's chest now.

"I did it to even the score over my partner's death, too. Garson is responsible for a whale of a lot."

"He'll get what's coming to him now," Caroline said. Her arms went around Slocum's neck and pulled his head down to hers so she could whisper, "And you should get what's coming to you, too!" She kissed him as hard as he kissed her. Slocum had received a few dollars reward from the stage company. This was a far better reward.

"I, uh, I have to see the marshal off. Be sure everything's in order, you understand." Horace Trevor fussed about for a few seconds, then came to a decision when he saw Slocum and Caroline were not breaking off their kiss. "I'll close the office. Lock up. Look after business, will you, Mr. Slocum?"

"You don't need to hurry back, Mr. Trevor," Caroline said, breaking off the kiss and licking her lips.

"I, uh, yes, of course." Trevor closed the door behind him and locked it. Caroline pulled down the blind on the door and turned back to Slocum.

"You deserve a *real* reward."

"The kiss wasn't the reward?" Slocum asked, unbuckling his gun belt and putting it on the counter.

"You know it wasn't." Caroline said, hiking her skirts and giving him a flash of the real prize. She came forward and pushed him back. Slocum stumbled and sat down heavily in a straight-backed chair. He started to get up, but Caroline pushed him back down.

"Don't," she said. "I saw how you're favoring that leg of yours. I guess Maybelle didn't fix it up right."

"That's not the leg that is bothering me," Slocum said. He unbuttoned his jeans and let his fleshy staff snap out.

"I can make that feel better, too," Caroline promised. She straddled his waist, got her skirts up high and then sank down on his lap.

Slocum grabbed the woman's hips and guided her as she lowered onto his manhood. The blood-engorged tip of his shaft brushed across her fleecy bush, then parted her lust-dampened nether lips. Caroline grinned as she felt the heat building.

"Are you ready?"

"I'm ready for the ride of my life," Slocum said. At least, he thought he was. Caroline lowered her full weight onto his lap, taking him fully up her moist, clinging female tunnel. He gasped at the sudden insertion. It felt as if he was being crushed all around in the most delightful way possible.

"You like it?" she asked in a husky voice.

Slocum looked up and saw that Caroline wanted more. So did he. Reaching over, he unfastened her blouse and let her snowy white breasts come tumbling out. Slocum pounced on the left breast, licking and kissing and suckling until Caroline groaned and began thrashing around. This caused his buried stalk to stir about deep within her, stimulating both of them even more.

Slocum sucked the hard cherry-red nub into his mouth and used his teeth gently. Every time Caroline shuddered, he thrust out his tongue and pushed the fleshy button down into the softness beneath until he felt the frenzied beating of her heart. Then he switched locations, moving to her other breast.

Caroline's arms circled his neck and pulled him closer. The shudders in her body as he stimulated her sensitive flesh built in intensity. Her hips bucked about and gave them both new lances of delight. Slocum let his hands rove over the woman's back and then down to her backside. Cupping the twin moons of her bare flesh, he began squeezing and kneading as if he had captured two lumps of dough.

This caused Caroline to writhe about even more. Both felt the avalanche of sensations deep in their loins, but Slocum fought to hold back the fierce tide mounting in his balls. He was pinned under her weight and unable to move because of the sturdy chair. That did not diminish his enjoyment. If anything, it caused his pleasure to soar even faster.

"Ca-can't do this much more," panted Caroline. "I'm on fire inside. You're so big. Throbbing inside me."

He began guiding her up and down in the motion he desired most, using the handfuls of rump to relay his intentions. She slid forward a bit on his lap, locked her ankles around the back legs of the chair and, using this for leverage, began rising and falling as fast as she could.

Slocum thought his loins had been set on fire. The friction of her body moving against his set off a real prairie fire that could not be stopped. She thrashed around, panting, moaning, crying out every time he kissed or licked her sensitive breasts. But the real action came from her lifting and dropping, taking him fully into her seething hot core.

"Oh, oh, ohhhh!" Caroline cried out. She threw her head back as she crammed her hips down hard. The chair creaked as Slocum sank an extra inch into her molten center. This was enough to set her off. He felt a powerful spasm of passion ripple through her body and crush down around his hidden length. Slocum tried to hold back, to enjoy even more, but Caroline's twisting and gyrating prevented it.

With her ankles hooked on the chair legs, she was able to pull herself down powerfully and grind her hips into his. Slocum tried to hold back the fierce tide boiling within, and then he let go. Caroline let out another gasp as her body shook anew. Then they both sagged, the tensions and pleasures gone for the moment.

"That was incredible, John," she said. They stared at each other for a few seconds, then Caroline grinned. "We need a bath."

"What do you have in mind?"

"I know this place out by the house where the water bubbles up into a pool. It's secluded and—"

"Race you there," Slocum said.

19

"I keep wondering why Garson didn't come to help when Dark Crow was attacking your house." Slocum said, stretched out on a hot rock like a lizard in the sun. Beside him Caroline stretched, yawned and looked lovely.

"He was an awful man," she said. "He wanted us dead."

"Why? Letting the Apaches kill you and your folks bought him nothing. If he ran off Dark Crow, he might have won a medal." Slocum frowned as he looked out over the desert, tracing the route Garson had taken. Once before, when he had injured his leg, Slocum had followed the officer to where his gang had camped. Garson had ridden with a company of buffalo soldiers and sneaked away from them then—and maybe he had done the same thing during Dark Crow's attack on the Thornton ranch.

"I think he used the soldiers as cover to go meet his gang—and to check his stash," Slocum said. "For all that, he might have used them as his personal bodyguards, and they never knew it."

"He certainly used the buffalo soldiers for menial tasks around the fort," Caroline said. "He treated them worse than slaves."

"What's in that clump of rocks yonder?" Slocum said,

pointing to the most likely spot where Garson would have ridden, if he had left his company for less than an hour.

"Just rocks. Nothing special."

"Let's ride over and take a look," Slocum said.

"Do you think we'll find something there?" From her eager question, Slocum knew that Caroline had caught gold fever.

"We won't know until we look," Slocum said, helping her up. They mounted and rode down to the desert, followed the mountains behind her parents' house to the foothills Slocum had singled out as worthy of investigation.

"There's nothing here, John," she said, looking around. "Nothing but a lot of rocks."

"A faint trail. It's not a game trail, either," said Slocum. "I can see where horseshoes have nicked rock as a horse made its way up there." He looked up into the boulders to a secluded spot invisible from out in the desert. He left Pappy behind and scrambled up, since the steep slope was covered with gravel.

"Wait, I want to see, too," called Caroline. She trailed him clumsily. Slocum would have waited for her or even helped, but he had caught more than a touch of gold fever himself. He saw more fresh scratches on the side of a large rock and hurried around it into a small hollow. Caroline pushed in behind him as he stood looking around.

"What have you found, John?" she asked breathlessly.

"It doesn't look like anything—but I'm not going to rush." Slocum circled the basin, seeing how spring runoff water poured over the largest of the rocks and drained through the sand-and-gravel bottom. This took him to the large rock and the way it hung out over the dirt. He dropped to his knees and began digging in the soft dirt underneath.

"It's not packed down," Caroline said. "Do you think— oh, John!"

Slocum dragged out a large strongbox and brushed it off. He looked up at Caroline, took a deep breath, then opened the box. The lid creaked metallically and then gave them both a sight that caused them to catch their breaths.

"I've never seen so much money," Caroline said.

"Gold coin, bags of dust, the sort of thing carried in stagecoach shipments."

"He was rich, John. Why would he be lured into robbing the stage when you set him up?"

"Greed. There's never enough for people like Garson."

"You reckon that money kin be 'dentified as comin' from the stage company?" drawled Corporal Donnelly. He pushed his way into the tiny hollow and looked at the glittering gold. Two more buffalo soldiers crowded in.

If Slocum had ever thought of keeping the gold for himself, it vanished in that moment.

"I do, Corporal," Slocum said, closing the lid. "How'd you happen to be out here?"

"Same as you, I s'pose, Mistah Slocum," Donnelly said. "Got to thinkin' on why the lieutenant rode on past when Dark Crow was 'tackin'. Even him's not that mean." Donnelly hesitated a moment, then smiled, saying, "He could have won a medal. For a man like him, that's most nearly as good as money."

"Almost," Slocum said, laughing. Donnelly thought along the same lines as he did. "Take the loot back to the fort and let Mr. Trevor know you found it."

"The lieutenant goes on trial tomorrow. Yer not meanin' to miss it, are you?" Donnelly asked.

"No," Slocum said simply. The two buffalo soldiers hefted the box and wiggled through the narrow passage with it. Donnelly saluted Slocum, then left.

"That was so much money," Caroline said. "I have an admission. I actually thought of keeping it. How selfish of me. And how foolish. That would make me just like Garson, wouldn't it?"

"Never," Slocum said. He fell quiet. Caroline stared at him until she couldn't stand the silence any longer.

"What are you thinking, John? That there's more money?" When he didn't answer, she worried on the problem a few seconds longer, then brightened. "The money he stole from the post! Do you think he spent it all?"

"There was too much. This was Garson's private treasure, gold he didn't share with the rest of his gang. I'll lay a wager there is another hoard somewhere of money he *did* share with them."

"Money he didn't care if some of the gang stole from him!"

"That would keep them loyal, and he wasn't losing anything because he had gold and . . ."

Together they said, ". . . and they had greenbacks."

"This is where you fell?" Caroline asked, looking up at the towering cliffs. She shuddered. "You're lucky to be alive."

"I am," Slocum agreed, glancing at her. They had squeezed through the narrow crevice Slocum had used before. He had seen the smears of his dried blood along the rocks but had not pointed that out to her. The small canyon bottom was dotted with cottonwoods and spindly pines he had not noticed before in the dark—except when he had crashed through their limbs.

"That's where I spied on Garson and his gang," Slocum said, going to the clearing with the firepit. "I didn't chase them off. They camped here often, from the look of the debris around." Garson and his men had not been too tidy in their camp, which might explain why the cougar had been willing to attack Slocum. It had dined well on the garbage left behind, and Slocum had disturbed it during a meal.

"He's not the kind to trust his men," Caroline protested. "I don't know them, but from what has been said, any of those outlaws would steal the money and never think twice about it."

"Garson had enough presence to command his men on this point. He might have held them in the gang by promising to divvy up all the take—but it was not likely he would share gold with them." Slocum hunted for a spot where paper money might be hidden.

An hour later, he found a rock that had been moved repeatedly. Rolling it aside revealed two planks. He yanked them free and showed a three-foot-deep pit stuffed with canvas bags.

"That's all money?" Caroline asked incredulously.

"Seems to be," Slocum said, ripping open one bag after another, spilling out the scrip. "Most of it is worthless. Paper money on banks in El Paso or Santa Fe that nobody'd take here."

"But there's plenty on the Mineral Springs and Mesilla banks," she said. "Thousands of dollars."

"Most of it has been stolen from the fort," Slocum guessed. "There's no telling how long Garson was overcharging the Army for the post supplies."

"So this belongs to the Army, too," Caroline said sadly. Slocum knew the reason for her melancholy—and how to cure it.

"There's no way the Army can use this money to replace the supplies Garson cheated the soldiers out of. That's water over the dam. But someone who knew what the soldiers needed in the future could put this money to real good use. Like you. Like Maybelle Washington."

Caroline brightened. She rushed to him and hugged him.

"And," Slocum said, eyeing the rest of the greenbacks,

"I might be in Santa Fe or El Paso someday and be able to use *that* money."

The court-martial for Garson and Porter had drawn senior officers from surrounding forts. There was enough gold braid sitting at the judges' table to blind Slocum with reflected sunlight. The mess hall was crowded and many were forced to stand outside in the hot sun and peer through doors and open windows to see the proceedings. Slocum almost wished he were with them rather than in the burning hot hall.

Major Cavendish rapped for silence.

"The charges against Lieutenants Garson and Porter have been read and arguments presented. It is my duty to read the verdict reached by the members in the trial." Cavendish opened a folded paper, then placed it carefully in front of him on the table.

"Guilty," Caroline whispered. "It can't be anything else."

Slocum knew the Army had the two officers dead to rights. What he wanted to hear was the sentence. If Garson didn't swing . . .

He touched the butt of his Colt Navy. Curt Degraff might not rest easier in his grave if Slocum ended Garson's miserable life, but Slocum would feel he had done his duty.

"This court-marital finds you both guilty as charged," Cavendish said.

"Wait!" shouted Porter, leaping to his feet. Soldiers moved in to keep him from escaping. "I didn't do any of the killing! It was all Garson's doing!"

"The time for such arguments in your defense was during the court-martial," Cavendish said coldly.

"I know where Dark Crow is camped! I'll show you, if you don't hang me!"

A buzz went through the crowd.

"Shut up, you fool!" shouted Garson. "That's the only hole card we have!"

"We will find Dark Crow, with or without your aid. But you are saying in open court that you have known where the Apaches are hiding and did nothing about it?"

"The Floridas. In the Florida Mountains forty miles south of here. There's a small canyon on the north side. Dark Crow and his renegades are there!" Porter cried.

"Thank you for your help," Cavendish said coldly. "It does not mitigate your sentence."

"You fool," growled Garson. "We don't have anything to bargain with now!" He tried to grab Porter, but two buffalo soldiers forced him back down into his chair.

"The verdict of this court is that you shall both be hanged by the neck until dead. Sentence will be carried out three days hence, at noon." Major Cavendish rapped his gavel again, then huddled with the other officers. Slocum didn't have to hear what was said to know they were going to send scouts out to see if Porter had told the truth.

"Mr. Slocum," said Maybelle Washington, coming through the crush in the mess hall. "I want to thank you."

"For what?" he said. Slocum felt guilty that he had not been able to get evidence that Garson—and probably Porter—had been responsible for her husband's cruel death.

"Private Monroe's wife had a passel of doctor bills. They've been paid, thanks to you."

Slocum looked at Caroline, who beamed. The first of the greenbacks they had found had been put to good use.

"A supply of flour without weevils is on the way from Mesilla, too," Maybelle said.

"I'm glad. You have everything well in hand."

"I wish there had been more we could do for you," Maybelle said.

Slocum looked at the soldiers herding Garson and Porter from the mess hall. Retribution would come to them soon enough, probably not satisfying Slocum's need for revenge but at least forever preventing the two officers from future evildoing. Several hundred dollars in greenbacks issued by banks in El Paso rode in his pocket. Worthless here, valuable in the border city. And then he looked at Caroline.

"I've got all I need," Slocum said.

In a low voice, Caroline said. "And I'll be certain you get all you want!"

Slocum couldn't think of a better reward.

JAKE LOGAN

TODAY'S HOTTEST ACTION WESTERN!

TO ORDER CALL:

1-800-788-6262

(Ad # B110)

Watch for

SHOOT-OUT AT WHISKEY SPRINGS

278th novel in the exciting SLOCUM series
from Jove

Coming in April!